"It was a nice party," Meghan said. "You have wonderful friends and they care about you. Thanks for introducing me."

"You did all the work. I should be thanking you," Thomas replied.

For a moment they said nothing. The air between them changed, electrified. Thomas suddenly became much more aware of the way his hand was holding hers, the small amount of space that separated them. He felt like a teenager again, saying good-night to his first date and wondering whether it was appropriate to kiss her good-night.

With Meghan he knew it wasn't, but that didn't stop him from wanting to feel the softness of her mouth, taste the sweetness of her being. Feel her body pressed against his own.

Then she took matters into her own hands. Standing on her toes, she kissed his cheek. Without thinking, Thomas let his hands travel to Meghan's waist and gently brought her in closer. She moved her head back to look at him. Their mouths were only a kiss apart. Thomas felt her breath. He looked into her eyes, those beautiful eyes that drew him to her as if she were some exotic goddess.

For a moment Thomas thought he should say something, move away and break the connection that was holding them together, but he ignored it as he looked into Meghan's eyes again. He hadn't felt like this in a long while. And he liked it.

Books by Shirley Hailstock

Kimani Romance

Wrong Dress, Right Guy
Nine Months with Thomas

Silhouette Special Edition

A Father's Fortune
Love on Call

SHIRLEY HAILSTOCK

Shirley Hailstock began her writing life as a lover of reading. She liked nothing better than to find a corner in the library and get lost in a book, explore new worlds and visit places she never expected to see. As an author, not only can she visit those places, she can be the heroine of her own stories.

A past president of Romance Writers of America, Shirley holds a Waldenbooks Award for Bestselling Romance and a Career Achievement Award from *Romantic Times BOOKreviews*. She is a recipient of an Emma Merritt Award for service to RWA and a Lifetime Achievement Award from the New York City Chapter. Contact Shirley at shirley.hailstock@comcast.net, or visit her Web site at www.geocities.com/shailstock.

Nine
MONTHS
WITH
Thomas

SHIRLEY
HAILSTOCK

KIMANI
ROMANCE

To the

"Miracle Children"

All children are gifts and all children are miracles,
but those hard-won conceptions and births
are such a precious love.

And to Christopher
My own hard-won miracle child.

 KIMANI PRESS™

Recycling programs
for this product may
not exist in your area.

ISBN-13: 978-0-373-86110-1
ISBN-10:   0-373-86110-9

NINE MONTHS WITH THOMAS

Dear Reader,

Happy Mother's Day! I am so happy to be able to bring you a book about a mother-to-be. I love that line from *Gone with the Wind* when Melanie is talking to Rhett and tells him, "The best days are when babies come."

With the news reporting the increasing statistics related to teenage pregnancies, the plight of the infertile couple is often lost. It's not easy to want a child and be denied the pleasure of having one of your own. The emotions that Thomas and his wife went through are unimaginable to anyone who hasn't spent years working through the fertility process.

In *Nine Months with Thomas,* our hero finds himself at a fork in the road: he's lost his wife, but she left behind a single chance for him to have his own child. The decision to try surrogacy is often a controversial one. Most people and even some states (which is why this book is set in Maryland) line up on one side of the issue or the other. But like any issue, the stakes change when they hit home.

Thomas makes his decision to bring Meghan into his life. Meghan reared her sister after their parents died. She feels she's already given her progeny to the world. But nine months living together and Meghan carrying Thomas's child changes them both.

I hope you enjoy the journey over the *Nine Months with Thomas.* Please contact me at shirley.hailstock@comcast.net or visit my Web site at www.geocities.com/shailstock.

Sincerely yours,

Shirley Hailstock

Chapter 1

Something was wrong. Or at least different. Thomas Worthington-Yates pushed his dinner plate away and sat back in his chair. His gaze swung from his mother-in-law to his father-in-law and back again. The table was set with exquisite china and fine linen. The food was excellently prepared and beautifully presented. He'd arrived on time and Adam and Nina Russell greeted him with the same welcoming arms they had since he first appeared on their doorstep nine years ago, head over heels in love with their daughter, Ruth. Nothing was out of place or unexpected. Except the weird vibe that permeated the room.

"You don't like the food?" he asked.

Both of them looked at their plates, but neither took a bite to eat.

"The food is fine," Adam said.

"Then why aren't you eating it?" Thomas paused. "Are you feeling all right?"

"We're fine," Nina replied.

"What is it then?" he asked.

Nina lifted her eyelids to look at him, then quickly dropped them to stare at her plate of uneaten food.

"Nina? Adam?" he prompted.

"Thomas, we want to talk to you…" Nina stopped.

Thomas steeled himself. Never had his in-laws had a problem talking to him about anything. They were friends. More than friends. They were family. Nina and Adam weren't the stereotypical in-laws. They were more like his real parents. He was glad to have them. Since Ruth died, he'd remained close to them.

"What do you want to talk about?" Thomas asked, sitting back the way he did in his office overlooking the Baltimore Harbor.

"About a grandchild." The words came out in a rush.

Thomas closed his eyes for a moment and waited for the feeling of loss to wash over him. It came each time he thought of Ruth and what her death had robbed them of. The feeling of loss was there, lighter in intensity than it had been at the beginning, but still present. His chest felt hollow, as if his heart had been buried with his wife and was no longer part of his anatomy.

"I'm sorry," Thomas said, "I can't get pregnant right now."

"I know you meant that to be funny," Adam said. "But we're serious."

Thomas sat up in his chair, leaning forward on the table. His father-in-law's expression was serious, without a flicker of amusement. "What do you mean? You know I'm not seeing anyone seriously."

"We do," he said.

"And you know adoption is the only way I could possibly provide you with a child and that could take years."

"There's another way," Nina stated.

"What?" He looked from Nina to Adam. "What other way?"

That day two years ago came back to him. It was a perfect day. It was supposed to be a happy day, but it ended tragically, taking his wife, his unborn child and his ability to ever father another child. His in-laws knew that. They were the only ones who knew it.

"Thomas, don't get upset," Nina warned. She placed her hands on the table, straddling her plate, as if she needed to hold the mahogany wood to the floor.

Thomas waited. It took her a while. He wanted to shout at her to get it out, tell him what she was talking about.

"Surrogacy."

She'd spoken so softly, he could hardly hear her. "What did you say?"

"She said surrogacy," his father-in-law supplied, his voice strong and confident.

"Absolutely not!" Thomas exploded. He shot up from the chair, throwing his napkin on the table and leaving the dining room. The emptiness in his chest had become a rock. Now it weighed him down, forcing him to review what could have been, but now could never be. He needed a drink.

Thomas knew the Russells' home as well as he knew his own. He went straight to the library and subsequently to the bar. Filling a highball glass with ice, he added scotch and slung it to the back of his throat. Seconds later, his in-laws followed him.

"Think about it, Thomas," Nina continued. "This is the last chance we have of being grandparents. And it's your only chance to father a child of your own."

"Don't you think I know that?" He was rarely angry or harsh with the Russells, people he loved. While he'd never called them Mom and Dad, they were ideal in-laws, never butting into his marriage or pitting their daughter against him. When Ruth died, they were there supporting him, even though they were grieving as well. "I'm sorry," he apologized. "I didn't mean to sound so bitter. It's just that without Ruth…" He stopped, unable to finish the sentence.

"We met someone who is willing to be a surrogate." Nina said after a moment. "She doesn't want children of her own, and will sign a contract to carry your and Ruth's baby. You can even be at the birth then you take your baby home."

Thomas heard the hope in his mother-in-law's voice. He also realized they'd thought about this for a while. They'd even researched it to the point of finding and interviewing a surrogate. He wondered how long this had been going on and how many women they had talked to.

"If you don't want the child, we'll raise it." She offered him a solution to what she thought might be his misgivings.

"I would be part of my child's life," he said.

Nina's shoulders dropped in relief. He knew she thought her argument had been won. "Of course, you would. And you'd be a great father."

Thomas raised his hands, stopping whatever else she was about to say. "I don't want a surrogate."

"We'd stay in touch with her. We'd answer all her questions, go with her to doctor's appointments."

"She could even stay here with us," Adam suggested.

"I won't have it," Thomas said. "The two of you know you don't need that kind of stress in your lives."

"We can handle it," Nina told him.

"Like you did with Ruth?" He took a moment to gaze at both of them. "You were on pins and needles every day of each of our attempts to get pregnant. And Ruth had a better chance of success because she had several embryos that we froze. What would it be like with a surrogate and only one frozen embryo left?"

"Thomas, what about the embryo?" Adam asked. "You can't just let it sit there."

"I can," he said. "I don't have time to babysit a surrogate right now."

"We understand that you're a busy man," Nina said. "Adam and I are willing to take care of everything. You don't have to be involved if you don't wish to."

He stared at them both, then took another swallow of his drink. "You can't," he said.

"We know we can't do anything without your permission," Adam said. "But once that's given—"

"I'm not giving it." He slammed the glass down on the bar. Nina jumped slightly. Thomas saw the look of disappointment on their faces.

"Give it some time," his father-in-law said. "Give yourself time to get used to the idea. Talk to the woman. Think about holding your own child."

"Adam, Ruth and I tried for years. You know that. The doctors say you need more than one embryo to assure success and there is only one left. It would be foolish to have a surrogate, with all that entangles, when the chances of the embryo surviving are so low."

"They're low, but they're not zero," Adam said.

"Thomas, it's the only chance we have." Nina's voice was low and desperate.

"Promise me you'll think about it?" Adam asked.

"All right," he said. "I'll think about it. But don't get your hopes up."

Nina smiled for the first time that night. Thomas felt a little happier, too. He loved his in-laws the same way he had loved his parents. Nina and Adam both had heart conditions and Thomas didn't want anything to happen to them. He'd lost his parents—first his father to cancer and then six months later his mother died of a heart attack. After seven years of marriage, Ruth had died in a car accident. He had to admit his in-laws made some good points. He felt his heart beat a little faster.

"By the way, who is the surrogate carrier? And why'd she agree to do this?"

"Her name's Meghan Howard," Adam answered.

Thomas finished the rest of his drink with a single gulp. Could this night get any worse? he wondered. He had to fly to London in three hours and now he was dealing with people who wanted a legacy and wanted him to spend his free time with a woman he didn't know.

"How old is she?"

"She's thirty. Ruth was twenty-nine," her mother reminded him. "She would have been thirty when the baby was born."

If she had lived, Thomas thought. Her birthday was a month away when the accident happened. She was three months pregnant. Longer than any of the other pregnancies had lasted. And then the accident had taken everything. Or so he thought.

But now, there was a chance. One last chance. *Should he take it?* He hadn't thought about the last embryo. He'd known it was there. The promise of life he and Ruth had created. When she died, Thomas had given up. His unborn child had died with his wife. But now there was a chance. A slim chance. One last possibility. What would Ruth want him to do? He'd be a single father. Was he ready for that? he wondered.

Thomas poured another drink and took a sip. He focused on Ruth's face in his mind. He missed her. They'd had such plans. And life had played an awful trick on them. But she'd left behind one last chance for them. One embryo remained viable. His in-laws had brought the idea to his mind. He could still father Ruth's child, but did he have the courage to do what she'd want without her?

Day thirty of her job search, Meghan Howard thought. It was nearly noon and she was finally dressed. At least today was better than the last twenty-nine. And she had no job interviews to be humiliated by. Every company seemed to be downsizing. She was having

less and less luck finding positions and even worse luck
getting interviews. Social workers were not a necessity
it seemed. If she didn't find a job soon, she'd have to
move out of the city, maybe even the state. Everywhere
she went, people just weren't hiring.

She'd had one "job offer" from a middle-aged
woman and her husband. Meghan shuddered, refusing
to think about them. Their proposal was too outrageous
to consider.

*Who approaches a stranger in an office and asks
them to have their grandchild?*

Well, they weren't exactly in the office. She'd stepped into the office to ask for directions to her next job
interview. Even though she'd lived outside of Baltimore
all her life, there were areas of the city she'd never been
to. It was only as she left the office that she caught sight
of the wall of medical information. She'd seen the brochures and not seen them. Only when the couple started
talking did she realize that all the brochures and even
the posters on the walls had to do with surrogacy and
egg donation.

Meghan had left the office with her map in hand. The
couple followed her into the corridor and onto the
elevator. She nodded at the older woman as she stepped
aside to give her room. Forgetting them almost as soon
as the doors slid open, Meghan headed to the closest
coffee shop for a latte and to study the maps until it was
time to go to her next appointment. The couple had
come in behind her and sat at her table. To say it was a
memorable conversation would be like saying the polar
ice caps were made of wedding cake icing.

Now, glancing through the windows, Meghan saw the mailman. He was early today. She thought of leaving the mail in the box. All she got were bills and junk mail. Still, going to the mailbox gave her a moment when she didn't have to think of her current situation.

She sorted through the bundle of envelopes confirming her thoughts on its contents. The last one in the group was a square-shaped envelope from Suzanne. Meghan's heart lifted when she recognized her sister's handwriting.

She opened the cream-colored envelope in the living room and pulled out the card. On the cover was a photo of a mother holding her baby. "Happy Mother's Day" was written in script across the bottom. Meghan smiled, blinking away tears that clouded her eyes and made the words on the paper swim before her eyes. Meghan could hear Suzanne's voice as she read. Her sister could have been in the room, her voice was so clear.

You are not the mother of my body, but of my choice.
An accident of birth bonded us together.
You did not carry me for nine months, but for all
my life.
Happy Mother's Day.
Love, Suzanne.

Emotion rushed over Meghan, clogging her ears and making her heart beat faster. She sat down on the sofa. Reading the card a second and then a third time, Meghan laid it on the table and leaned back. Grabbing a throw pillow, she hugged it to herself, pulling her knees up to her chest.

Suzanne had been her life since their mother died. She was only twelve years old at the time. Meghan was twenty, just out of college and working her first job, but she refused to be separated from her sister.

Thankfully Suzanne was out of school now and had a job of her own. Of course, she was living clear across the country in California and working in television. With the cost of living out there and her entry-level salary, she couldn't afford to help Meghan out. And Meghan would never ask.

For years, she had been the caregiver and supporter of her younger sister. Suzanne was just starting her working life. Meghan would only let Suzanne know her situation if she had no other option. Right now, severance pay would cover her expenses for the next few months. Her savings, however, were extremely low. She'd been using every penny she had to educate her sister and pay the monthly bills.

Just when she thought she'd be able to save for herself and return to school—*bang*—she'd lost her job and her only source of income. The outrageous proposal came back to her. It was crazy to even consider it, she thought. Sitting on her sofa, Meghan recalled the conversation she'd had with the couple the day before.

"We saw you come out of the surrogacy agency," the woman had said. "And we recognized you. We went to a lawyer and he recommended that agency."

"Agency?"

They both nodded.

She'd gone into a nondescript office building to get directions.

"I'd never been there before," she'd said. "I only went in…"

"So this will be your first time? Have you already found another couple?"

Meghan had had no idea what they meant. "A couple for what?"

And then the bombshell dropped. She must have asked directions from a surrogacy agency's office. They'd thought she was a surrogate!

Meghan had laughed when she realized the mistake, but the expressions on Adam and Nina's faces had been serious. They'd proposed that Meghan be a surrogate mother for their baby—actually, their grandbaby.

Meghan picked up the Mother's Day card and read it again. As she laid it back on the table, the doorbell rang. Her brows went up and she looked at the door. She wasn't expecting anyone.

"Meghan Howard?" a man with dark eyes and killer good looks stood on *her* porch. At least it was *hers* for the time being. Very likely she'd have to move soon.

She nodded.

"Thomas Worthington-Yates," he said.

She knew who he was. And not just from the press. Though his face *had* stared back at her from *Time, Business Week, Black Enterprise* and many other magazines on the newsstands. He was the boy wizard, although "boy" was not apt description for the dashing, handsome man standing in her doorway.

He had broad shoulders and a tight waist. His

business suit was obviously made to order. The tie was raw silk and Meghan had to look up to see his face, which wasn't welcoming at all. His gaze was stern.

"I'd like to talk to you," he said.

"About what?" she asked. As far as she knew they had nothing in common, unless he wanted to give her a job. That she would be interested in. But she was a social worker. Did he do work that helped others?

"Would you mind if I come in?"

She took a step back and opened the door to him. He crossed the threshold and walked into the living room. He looked around, Meghan following his gaze as he took in the small room.

"Please sit," she offered. He took a single chair across from the sofa. "Would you like something to drink? I have fresh coffee, or tea, water."

He waved his hand, indicating no. "I'm fine," he said.

She could see that. He was a no-nonsense kind of man. He didn't waste time being cordial.

Meghan wondered if he remembered her. Was that why he was here?

For a moment there was silence. Why would the wizard of Wall Street be in her living room? she wondered. They looked at each other and both looked away. Meghan ground her back teeth. This was her house. She refused to let him intimidate her.

"Excuse me," she said, squaring her shoulders. "Why are you here?"

He leaned forward in the chair, clasping his hands together. Then he stood up and walked about the room. Meghan looked after him. She saw the room through a stranger's eyes. She'd been comfortable here. She and Suzanne had spent a lot of their lives in these rooms. Now she could see the shabby furniture, aged wallpaper, outdated color schemes. She felt like asking him to leave.

He turned back to her. "You met a couple the other day…" He stopped. "They're my in-laws."

She stiffened. He knew them, she thought. Did he know what they'd wanted with her?

"They were talking to me on your behalf?" she asked.

"Not exactly. They approached you without my knowledge."

Meghan sighed, letting out a long breath. "That's great. I guess you're here to apologize."

"Apologize?"

She was wrong. She should have known it. Men like Thomas Worthington-Yates didn't apologize. Especially to people like her. He probably thought *she* should be the one apologizing.

"I suppose they didn't need to apologize after I turned them down."

"You what?"

Her head snapped up at the intensity of his question.

"You turned them *down?*"

She nodded. "Didn't they tell you?"

"They told me you had agreed."

She sat back as if she'd been pushed. "To have someone else's baby? Why would I do that?"

"I don't know. They said you had a good reason. I assumed it was money." Again he glanced around the room. "They said you'd lost your job."

"I did. I mean, I lost my job. Budget cuts," she explained. "But losing my job doesn't mean I want to get pregnant. I don't even want kids. Why would I loan my body out to have one?"

Thomas faced her. He looked as if he wanted to say something, but chose to keep it to himself. "I'm afraid I've wasted both our time." The comment was obviously a dismissal. Thomas headed for the door. Meghan followed him. He walked as if he owned the house and she was the one being seen to the door.

"Why do you want to do this?" she asked.

"I don't," he said. "My in-laws want to be grandparents. They asked me to come and see you. I agreed."

"If it's only for your in-laws, why would you come to see me, even assuming you thought I'd agreed?"

"It would have been an interview," he said.

"So you are considering it?"

"I don't know."

She had the feeling he wasn't used to being questioned.

"Look, I agreed to come and talk to you on their behalf. It was a mistake. I'm leaving," he said and turned back to the door.

"What are you going to do now?" she asked, unsure why she wanted to know.

"Nothing."

"Are you sure?"

"Where is this going?" he asked.

"Only you can answer that," she told him. Meghan had been in social work long enough to understand that what people said was overshadowed by what they did. A man like Thomas Worthington-Yates, someone as busy as he was, someone who didn't go to see subordinates, but had them come to him, was not standing in her doorway unless deep inside him he really wanted this child.

"What do you mean?" he asked.

"I mean you want this child. You can delude yourself as much as you want. For whatever reason you're putting up roadblocks. Your in-laws may have instigated the situation, but they didn't force you into a car and drive you over here. You came to see, not to find out if I would do it, but if *you* could."

"Thank you, Dr. Freud. I'll make an appointment with your receptionist on my way out."

He turned and strode away. Meghan watched him through the screened door. It was her job to observe human nature. Thomas walked straight toward his expensive sedan sitting at the curb, its gold accents gleaming in the afternoon sun. But he wasn't as cocksure as he had been when he arrived. She'd touched a nerve.

And he didn't seem to like it, not one bit.

Chapter 2

She refused. What right had she to refuse to carry his baby, he thought. Thomas slammed the car door as he got inside and started the engine. *Look at her. Look at where she lives.* Being unemployed, she should have jumped at the chance.

But she refused.

Thomas wasn't used to people turning him down. When he requested something be done, it was done. He ran his own investment business and he did it well. People came to him to manage their money. He was only asking Meghan to join his staff, be another employee.

Yet she'd refused.

Well, Thomas thought, there were other women. She wasn't the first woman, and she wouldn't be the last. He pulled away from the curb and within minutes had joined the traffic headed across the harbor and back downtown. He was in his office within minutes and punching in the phone number of his in-laws with enough force to shatter the electrical mechanism under the surface of the phone.

Nina appeared on the wide video screen on his wall. In addition to wiring the Russell's house to alert medical services if they had an emergency, a videophone had been installed in their home after she and Adam had heart attacks and refused to hire private nurses. Thomas could see if there were any signs that they needed help and alert the medical services, if needed.

Now, however, he wanted to ream them out as if they were little children who'd done something horribly wrong.

"You forgot to mention one very important item about Meghan Howard."

Adam came into view. Thomas knew Adam had heard the anger in his voice and came to support his wife. Ruth would have done the same.

"She refused," Thomas said. "Meghan Howard had no idea why I was there. She thought everything had been settled when she told you no."

"Thomas, don't get upset," Nina said placatingly. "She may have not been willing in the beginning, but with time to think over the proposition, I'm sure she'll agree."

"Nina, you're not listening. The woman does not want children, her own or anyone else's."

"I'll talk to her."

"No," he exploded. "You won't." Feeling bad for his outburst, Thomas lowered his voice. "Nina, Adam, this is obviously a volatile subject. Let's take a step back and not discuss it now. We need some distance."

"All right," Adam said.

Thomas used this method as a business practice. When more time was needed for a decision, he'd give it a few days. Think about it, put things into perspective. Why he hadn't done this before he dialed the phone, he didn't know.

"Why don't you come to dinner on Thursday and we'll talk about it again."

Thomas reviewed his calendar. If he had an appointment scheduled for that evening he'd cancel or reschedule it. This subject was obviously important to his in-laws. He didn't want to make it appear that he was putting them off. And if he was honest, it was beginning to be important to him, too.

"Thursday," he said. "See you then."

"Goodbye," Nina said, and pressed the button that broke the connection.

The screen went black and he saw his reflection standing in the middle of his office. He'd been pacing the floor. Thomas wasn't a nervous man, but he seemed to have a lot of energy now that needed an outlet. He'd go to the gym tonight.

Going to his desk, he sat down and tried to work. The image of Meghan Howard swam before his eyes. She was tall and thin, but not too thin. She had beautiful eyes. He'd watched their brown depths flash when she realized he was there about her surrogacy. Her

long hair was a mass of ringlets hanging past her
shoulders. Thomas had the irrational thought of
pushing his fingers into that mass, especially when
she stood and the sun shining through her living room
windows highlighted the red that wove through the
dark brown color.

Why does she look so familiar? Thomas felt the beginnings of attraction. He dashed it away, knowing he
hadn't felt anything like that since he'd first seen Ruth.

Meghan had asked him what he was going to do
now. Thomas didn't know. His office was on the twenty-
seventh floor of the Financial Center Building, overlooking the Baltimore Harbor. He stared, unseeing, at
the traffic. He was staring into the small house where
Meghan lived. He could see her tall figure, her jeans
tight and formfitting.

Thomas could just as soon cup her bottom in the
palms of his hands.

"You are losing it, man," he told himself.

He'd thought of going to the gym tonight, after work.
But that was too far ahead. He was going now!

The place was imposing to say the least, Meghan
thought as she stood in front of the house where Thomas
Worthington-Yates lived. It was just like him, worthy of
three names. The place wasn't exactly a mansion, but
she was sure there must be seven or eight bedrooms. Her
miniature house would fit inside it three or more times.

The house was redbrick and spanned the front of a
circular driveway. The lawn was manicured. A weed
would be tried, found guilty and executed without remorse

or appeal options, if it dared to mar the surface of this proud land. Flowers abounded all the way to the door.

Meghan couldn't help smiling at them. She loved flowers. They always brightened her day. Walking up the driveway, she saw no car, but there was probably a garage in the back, maybe even one of those old ones with an apartment above it for the chauffeur.

The bell played several notes before it stopped. With all this house, Meghan couldn't imagine Thomas living here alone. The place would need a staff to maintain it. But this was the shore.

"Meghan?"

Thomas blinked several times as he looked at her. Meghan knew she was the last person he expected to find on his doorstep out here where she could smell the salt in the air, but she had come here on a whim.

"You came to see where I lived," she said, with a slight lift of her left shoulder. "I thought I'd do the same. May I come in?"

Thomas stepped back. Meghan could tell he hadn't expected to see her again. The same was true of her. She'd have bet good money two days ago that she wouldn't be standing here. But changes had developed and it seemed his offer looked better and better.

"May I get you something to drink?" he mimicked her earlier offer. "Coffee, tea, water…"

She cut her eyes at him. "A margarita would be nice."

"With or without salt?"

"With."

"Follow me."

He led her through a foyer that lifted to the roof of

the house. Each succeeding room was equally impressive. It was light, bright and airy. She liked it, but wouldn't tell him that.

When they reached the library, equipped with a receding bar that folded back into the wall, she took one of the stools that magically appeared.

"If you ever give up this place, it can double as a museum. I would have said a school for troubled teens, but your neighbors would probably die of shock if that happened."

"I'll think about that, *if* the need arises."

"Which you doubt," she finished for him.

Behind the bar, he opened a refrigerator and pulled out lime wedges and ice. They were already cut, waiting for someone like her to drop by. On the wall behind him, he took down a bottle of tequila and Triple Sec as if his hands knew exactly where they were placed. He mixed the drink, poured it into a wide-mouthed glass that he'd rung with salt and slid it across the polished surface to her.

Pouring a second one, without salt, he lifted it for a toast. They clinked glasses.

"What are we toasting?" she asked.

He searched the room for an answer, then let his gaze rest on her. Meghan felt a twinge of guilt when he did that.

"To strangers," he answered.

They drank.

"We're not exactly strangers," she said when she placed her glass on the bar.

"We've met?"

"I was in the third grade and you were in fourth. I

believe your class and mine were seated together when we ended up at the science center. You called me a little squirt."

"Oh, my God. You're *that* Meghan Howard? I knew you looked familiar," he said. "You talked all through that presentation. And you kept hitting me on the arm to get my attention," he said and smiled.

"You didn't like it," she said. "Then when we were in high school, we met at a party. We even danced together. Of course you did it on a dare."

"I think I remember…"

"I wasn't very popular, but I wasn't stupid," she told him. She dropped her head a moment remembering that she was the homely girl and the class hunk had been dared to dance with her. "When it was over you couldn't get away from me fast enough."

"I'm sure I had a reason," he said.

"Emily MacLean," she answered. "You were interested in her."

"She's married now, lives in Ohio. Has three kids and runs a yarn shop."

Meghan smiled. She didn't know Emily MacLean. Emily went to the same high school as Thomas. They lived on the eastern shore and she lived in Baltimore. She'd been visiting a friend for the weekend while her mother was away when the party happened. He'd been called "Worth" then by his friends. Meghan didn't know he'd grow up to be the Thomas Worthington-Yates.

"Now that we've taken the trip down memory lane, why are you here?"

"I want to accept your offer." She buried her face in the huge glass, so he couldn't see her expression.

"What? Why the change of heart?"

"I spoke with your in-laws. They explained the situation in more detail."

She saw him visibly stiffen.

"What did they tell you?"

"How much you really wanted to have a child. How long you and your wife tried to have a baby and that this is your last chance."

His shoulders seemed to drop. Meghan had the feeling there was something more.

"That was all?"

"That was all," she stated. "Was something left out that I should know?"

He shook his head. He couldn't believe it. "What did they promise you?"

"A rent-free place to stay, medical care and all expenses related to the pregnancy paid. A few months before the child is born, I find an apartment. They pay the security deposits and the first six months rent. By then I should have a job and be able to support myself."

"Is that all?"

"And a substantial increase to my bank account, a surrogate's standard fee."

He nodded. "Where is this rent-free place?"

"With them."

"No," he said. The comment was as matter-of-fact as if he were asking her for the salt.

"Why not?"

"They both have heart conditions. They don't need to be stressed out every day by having you underfoot."

"I won't stress them out."

"You won't have to. Your presence will do that. You'll stay here."

"Oh, no," she said. "I think I'll just stay where I am. You can pay the rent there."

"No," he said. "I'll need to know that you're safe. That isn't the best neighborhood where you live. And you'll have everything you need here."

Meghan wondered about him. This was too easy. According to the Russells, Thomas needed to be convinced that this was a course he should take. But he'd fallen right in with the plan. Meghan wondered if she should be concerned. She knew things were never this easy.

"Medical expenses, an apartment," he said. "Seems fair in that you'll be giving up the one you have."

"So do we have a deal?"

"Not yet," he said. "There are some conditions. You will be signing an agreement regarding the medical procedure and parentage of the child. You'll be turning over the baby at birth."

"Agreed," she said without hesitation. "I've already given my progeny to the world."

"You have a child?" Surprise was evident in his question.

"My sister," she answered. "I reared her after our parents died. I told you, I have no wish to have children."

"I want to be clear that there will be no changing your mind after the event."

"I'm clear." She took another sip of her drink. "Anything else?"

He shook his head.

"Good, now my conditions."

His eyes opened a little wider. Obviously, he didn't think she'd have conditions. After all, she'd be pampered for nine months. And she'd be walking away with enough money to start a new life.

"I'm open-minded," he said, crossing his arms. "Shoot."

"When this is over, I want a job."

"A job?" He laughed. "We don't exactly employ social workers at my company. What do you propose to do?"

"Just something that will pay the rent and buy food and that involves helping people in some kind of way."

Thomas slipped off the bar stool. He moved around the back, but didn't make another drink. He placed his glass there and walked to the center of the room.

"You're going to get a windfall of money. Why do you need a job, too?"

"It's not that much money. And I have a use for it."

"Which is?" he asked, his eyebrows raising.

"I plan to return to school, earn my master's degree and go into counseling."

He nodded. "It's a noble use of the money."

"It won't be enough for both school and support. That's why I'll need a job."

"All right. You'll have a job."

Silence settled between them. Meghan had one more condition and it was a deal breaker.

"Is that all?" Thomas asked as the silence grew palpable. He was starting to get excited. He had given up on his dream and now it just may come true.

"There's one more thing."

"What is it?" She thought she saw him brace himself.

She swallowed. For a moment she couldn't speak. She never thought she'd be in a position of uttering this word. Of course, she expected someone would ask her. But this situation was like nothing she'd ever thought would happen either.

"Meghan, what is the condition?"

"Marriage."

Chapter 3

"What did you say?" Thomas asked. He would have taken a step toward her or one to sit down, if his legs had been capable of moving. Meghan Howard had done what no one in his life had ever been able to do before, rendered him immobile.

"Marriage." She'd said it again. Her eyes were steady. She hadn't moved from the barstool since she sat down. One arm lay across the bar, the other propped on the arm of the stool. Her long legs were crossed with one foot resting on the footrest. She was as calm as if she'd just told him she needed to brush her hair or change her shoes.

"You want me to marry you?"

"It's a deal breaker," she said. "I will not have a baby out of wedlock."

"But it's not your baby. It's a frozen embryo made up of my sperm and my deceased wife's egg."

"Doesn't matter. I'll be pregnant. I made a promise to myself years ago, and I'm standing by it."

Thomas moved, finding his legs now worked. He walked to where she sat. She watched him approach, but she didn't move. In the long run, she'd probably make a great counselor, as she had the ability to not let her true feelings show on her face. Thomas wondered what she was thinking. He wanted to know where and why she'd made this promise. Then it hit him.

"You were born that way," he stated.

"Illegitimately," she supplied.

It didn't sound as if she was afraid of the word, more like she was challenging him to say it, think it.

"And I promised myself I'd never have a child go through what I did."

"What was that? There's little stigma to the child, or the parent for that matter, these days."

For the first time, Meghan moved. She got down from the stool and crossed the room. She looked at the books in the bookcases, the fireplace, her body slowly moving around the room. Her hand ran across the leather chairs. Thomas wondered if she was taking in the luxuries she had missed as a child.

What also caught his attention was the way she moved. She no longer wore the tight jeans she'd had on when he stood in her living room. She had exchanged them for a yellow summer dress with a short-cropped jacket. Her yellow purse lay on the bar next to her drink. Her legs were long and shapely, accentuated by a pair of high heels. Thomas looked her up and down. How could he have ever thought she was homely? he wondered.

"It wasn't a stigma," she began, just when he thought she wasn't going to answer his question. "At least not one that people spoke of. It was evident in the invitations, parties, group trips."

"How?"

"Father-daughter camping trips, Career Day, Parent's Day, you name it." She shrugged. "A lot of the kids brought their fathers. The few who didn't have a dad, like me, were absent those days. I participated, but I was alone." She stopped. "My mother came when she could and I blessed her for being both parents, but it made me feel even worse when the men would gather together and leave her out."

"I'm sorry you had to go through that." Thomas was genuinely sorry. His father and mother came to every parent event that he had. It never occurred to him how it felt to be alone. He couldn't imagine what it was like for someone to have no one in the audience cheering them on.

"So you understand?"

"Not quite. After the baby is born, you'll be out of its life. It makes no difference if we're married or not."

"It makes a difference. And it'll make a difference to him or her later on to know that their parents were married when he or she was born."

"Meghan." Thomas spread his hand in exasperation. "You're not the mother. This makes no sense."

"Don't you get it?" she shouted. "It doesn't have to make sense. It's how I feel." Her hand went to her chest.

Turning away from him, she paced the room, walking back and forth several times, taking deep breaths. "I told your in-laws this wouldn't work."

"You've talked to them?" He stiffened. "They're in on this?"

Taking a deep breath, she faced him. "We had lunch. I came here from their house. I should have gone home, forgotten about this idea. It's preposterous anyway."

With determined steps, she went to the bar where she'd left the matching yellow purse. Grabbing it, she hooked it over her shoulder. "You were right," she said. "We are wasting each other's time."

She was leaving. Thomas had to stop her. It wasn't rational, he knew. And he didn't do irrational things. His life was made up of assessing situations from all angles and then making the best decision he could. Some of it was instinct. And right now his instinct told him to stop her.

He hadn't yet decided on the surrogacy, despite this interview and his apparent acceptance of the situation. But he wanted, for some unexplained reason, to keep her here and hear what she had to say.

One reason he listened to her was that he did really want his own child. Adam and Nina had brought it up, but it had taken root in his mind and now germinated. He understood that there were thousands of children who needed homes, needed adoptive parents that would love them, but that didn't negate his need to have his own child. To know that his blood ran in another's veins. That he had a legacy to leave the world. To know that he and Ruth could still create a miracle. Sundays in the park, horseback riding, camping, baseball games and teaching him his business—all these bonding moments, the patience and fortitude his father had taught him flooded through his mind. He had so much to give.

"Meghan," he called.

Her hand on the doorknob, she stopped and looked back. Her eyes were a little glassy, as if she was holding back tears, but her chin was regal.

"Look," she said. "It's a take it or leave it proposition. I won't budge on this."

This is the point where Thomas would normally throw someone out of his office. To him, take it or leave it meant leave it. But he curbed his tongue. For some strange reason, Meghan intrigued him. She had principles and no matter what she would not compromise them.

She wasn't the only person on the planet who would be willing to be a surrogate for him. He could always find someone else. Someone who wouldn't complicate an already unusual situation with a marriage based on nothing.

"You're not a real surrogate, are you?"

"I don't know what a real surrogate is," Meghan answered.

"You've never done this before," he stated. "I can't imagine someone marrying because she agreed to carry a baby and then give it away."

"You're welcome to find another host."

Meghan wasn't bluffing. Thomas could tell that from her expression and the way she'd sidestepped the question.

"I won't pretend to understand your logic," Thomas told her. "But suppose, and I said suppose, I agree to this marriage? Why is it so important to you?"

"If you think I'm trying to shake you down or somehow force you to stay married to me after the child, you're wrong."

"I wouldn't let it happen anyway," he said.

"When your son or daughter is thirteen or fourteen, it'll ask how it was possible that its mother was…wasn't alive when it was born, but she didn't die in childbirth. The child will want all the particulars."

"And I'll tell her or him. But saying the word surrogate rather than wife makes no difference."

"It will."

"By that time, I could be remarried and the child will only have known one mother."

"You said you never plan to remarry."

He took a deep breath.

"I know this is frustrating. The logic isn't there. It has to do with feelings, not something you could put into columns and rows and have all the down totals and cross totals come up to the same number. We're talking about lives, about people. Like love, logic has nothing to do with it."

For a long moment, Thomas said nothing. He was thinking her proposal. Maybe it wouldn't be so bad, Thomas thought. A wedding ring would deflect some of the husband-hunting women he met. He'd been written up in *Ebony* as a rich widower and it had brought throngs of unmarried women throwing themselves at him. Being an eligible bachelor had its advantages, but it also had its drawbacks. When he added the words financial tycoon to the picture, the drawbacks were inconvenient. Meghan could act as a decoy. But her having his baby as a surrogate opened him to both ridicule and constant speculation. As his pregnant wife, he could avoid all that. This just might work, he thought.

He was no saint, but the women he saw knew where his priorities lay. He didn't play games of deception, allowing them to think there was a chance to become the next Mrs. Worthington-Yates.

"There would be a prenuptial agreement," he stated.

"Of course," she agreed. She stared at him, her eyes steady. She was beautiful. And possessed the exact qualities he looked for when interviewing a possible employee. He wanted a person who was confident, sure of herself, knew that she could do the job, knew she would stand behind the decisions she made.

Meghan was all that. He could see it in the line of her body, the tilt of her head and the attitude apparent on her face. She was direct, and he usually hated that in a woman. But with her, it had been a refreshing change from being surrounded by people who agreed with everything he said.

"Now, why is that?" his dad would have said. He was always having Thomas analyze his actions. Thomas missed his gentle guidance. But even his dad couldn't advise him on this course of action.

"So what are you saying?" she asked. "You'll marry me?"

"You'll have to agree to a background check," he said.

"You mean an investigation?" Her brows arched. Thomas's eyes followed the perfect half-circles above her dark brown eyes.

"I have to be sure—"

"As do I," she interrupted. Again there was the directness, the surprise that he hadn't expected. "A man in your position needs to know what kind of crackpot he's dealing with," she said.

"I wouldn't call you a crackpot."

"Not right off the bat." Her eyes softened, taking the sting out of her words. "I assure you I have no skeletons in my closet, but you're looking for more than skeletons."

"I am?"

"Be honest with me. You're wondering what kind of woman is willing to go through childbirth with another woman's baby."

"The thought has crossed my mind."

"It's simple. I need a job with benefits."

"I'm sure there's more to it than that."

She walked back into the room and sat down. This time on the sofa.

"I'm thirty years old," she began. "All my life I've given to others. Don't get me wrong, I did it because I chose to do it. And I'm sure I will go on doing that, but I need more credentials. This will allow me to get them in half the time and without having to work night and day."

"And in a way, it's still giving to someone else," he said.

She cocked her head and thought for a moment. "I suppose you could think of it that way."

The smile that seemed to come from her heart was bright and genuine.

"At first I was against the idea. I'd never have come up with it on my own. Your in-laws approached me and I've had time to research the idea. I went back to that agency where they saw me and spoke with the counselors. Apparently there is a large number of people who do this."

"Are you planning to join them?"

She shook her head. "But if you want to forget about me and find someone who's a professional at this, I can give you the name of the agency."

"That won't be necessary," he said. Speaking with her had been a difficult enough interview, he couldn't imagine going through this with several candidates.

"Then are we agreed?" she asked.

"You'll have the baby and give it up? No strings?"

"There are plenty of strings," she said. "But none related to custody of the child."

"Then we have a deal."

"Well, where do I sign?"

"Papers will be drawn up by my attorney."

"Mine, too."

He stopped and stared at her.

"What's the matter?" she asked. "Didn't you think I'd want to know what kind of crackpot I'm dealing with?"

For a long moment Thomas Worthington-Yates stared at Meghan. He wondered if there were other women like her. She threw him off balance just when he thought his footing was sure. And he liked it. He smiled. That turned into a chuckle and then into a deep belly laugh.

Be careful what you wish for.

The cliché had Meghan laughing out loud. Sipping a cup of coffee, she tucked her legs beneath her and looked out on the street where she lived. It was her neighborhood. She and Suzanne had lived here for over a decade, but in a few days she'd be leaving it, never to return. The house sat close to the street, only a four-foot wide sidewalk separating it from the roadway. There were no trees or shrubs, only concrete and blacktop. A few houses, like hers, had window boxes with hanging flowers or green plants to break up the starkness of the uniform brick, but the place was nothing like the rolling lawns and manicured hedges of Thomas's home.

Meghan had wished for a job with better pay and she was getting it. Plus she was really truly helping someone. She laughed again, the same way she'd done in her car returning from Thomas's house. Many people appeared to talk or laugh in their cars. Most were on cell phones and no one paid any attention, but Meghan imagined people were casting curious glances her way. She sobered and concentrated on the traffic.

She was engaged.

Meghan tried to make sense of the statement. The proposal wasn't ideal. She had no ring and no mention of one was made by either her or Thomas. He hadn't even offered her his hand to shake. Their agreement had been more like a business merger than an engagement. There was no love, no show of happiness, no kiss. A handshake would have sealed the deal, but she thought it would be in poor taste. Maybe Thomas did, too.

The agreement hadn't been anywhere near the idealized version of a proposal, the stuff of her teenage dreams. That was back when she had dreams. When her mother was still alive. Things were tight for them. There was little money for Meghan to go school, so she worked her way through Morgan State, staying at home and commuting in a 1939 classic convertible with a leaky roof and floorboards you could see through. The car had died the day after graduation. Meghan knew it had been held together by need, hope, sweat and her will.

Her mother had worked days and nights to pay the meager tuition and keep food on the table. Then she died abruptly of a heart attack on her way to work a year after Meghan graduated and started work. They'd thought that with their combined incomes, they would be finally able to have some of the things they needed and wanted. And Suzanne wouldn't have the same financial restraints that Meghan had. But that dream ended, too.

Thomas. Now there was a dream. He was gorgeous, more of a hunk now than he'd been in high school when sexiness oozed from his biceps. But now there was a sadness about him, too. Meghan thought it had been brought on by the loss of his wife.

The phone rang and she set her cup on the window seat. She'd left several messages for Suzanne and was expecting a call back. But when she picked up the phone Thomas's secretary was on the other end of the line.

"He had to be in the District this morning and wondered if you would meet him for lunch?"

"In D.C.?"

"In Chevy Chase, actually. I can send a car for you."

"That won't be necessary." Meghan was a little pissed at his assumption that she had nothing to do but wait for him to send a car for her. "Where am I to meet him?"

"At *Chavalier's* on—"

"I know where it is," she interrupted. *Chevalier's* was the most expensive restaurant in Montgomery County.

"Did he say what time?" Meghan asked flatly.

"Noon."

Meghan heard no censure in her voice and felt a little guilty for the way she'd responded. It wasn't her fault that Thomas had farmed out a duty that he should have done himself.

"Thank you. I'll be there."

Hanging up the phone, Meghan checked the clock on the mantle. Suzanne had given her the small clock for Christmas last year. Meghan had only a couple of hours to get dressed and drive to the exclusive D.C. suburb. The distance wasn't that great if there was a straight line to get there, but she had to get through traffic, which was always congested.

She walked into the restaurant ten minutes late. Thomas stood up as the waiter showed her to his table. He looked perturbed. Meghan got a little satisfaction out of that. He'd had a secretary arrange a lunch with his fiancée and had given her barely enough time to get here. Her time was worth something too, she thought.

His face changed slightly as she got closer. Then it occurred to her that he might have changed his mind. He'd had her come here so he could tell her in the clear light of day that he wasn't willing to go through with it.

Meghan straightened her shoulders and lifted her chin. No loss, she told herself. Nothing had happened. Nothing physical. Nothing that couldn't be undone, un-thought. And if Thomas had gone squeamish on the idea, she'd rather know now than later.

"Hello," she said, refusing to apologize for the time.

He leaned over and kissed her cheek. Meghan was too stunned to do anything but stand there. A wave of emotion shot through her like a heat wave.

"I thought we should talk," he said.

"You've changed your mind." It was a statement.

"I haven't," he said.

Meghan felt relief, although she wasn't sure why.

"Have you changed yours?"

She shook her head.

"Good, then let's have lunch." He smiled and she studied his eyes. Obviously, Thomas could turn the charm on when he wanted to. Several people dropped by to shake hands with him. He introduced her by name, but gave no additional information about her status. Meghan didn't know how she would feel if he had said she was his fiancée.

They ordered and waited for their food to arrive. Whatever reason Thomas had asked her to come, he didn't bring it up initially. They talked about how exciting the capital was, how long she'd lived in Baltimore, where she'd gone to college and Suzanne.

"Was there something specific you wanted to discuss?" she asked after the salads had been served.

"I thought we ought to get to know each other better."

"You think we can do that over lunch?" She tried for lightness. "So where do you want to start?"

He didn't immediately answer. Meghan began to wonder if he'd heard her. Then wondered if he was going to answer.

"This can't be what you expected," he finally said.

She had no idea what he meant. "I expected a salad, a meal, coffee and dessert. Is there something I'm missing?"

He smiled. Meghan wondered why her heart suddenly skipped a beat.

"I meant the engagement. Didn't you dream of moonlight and soft music, someone saying 'I love you'?"

"Was that how it was when you proposed to Ruth?"

He glanced down at his salad, pushed it around and looked back up at her. He shook his head. "We were in college. It was homecoming." He smiled as he remembered it. "We'd won the football game."

"Were you on the team?" she asked.

"Me? I was a business school major. Didn't have the brawn for football."

He didn't have to play football, she thought. He was all right the way he was. He still had his boyish good looks, although his face held more character than it had when they were in high school.

"Ruth was in the queen's court. She looked gorgeous on the float. Her gown was yellow and looked as if it was made of flowers. She had yellow flowers in her hair and with all the flowers on the float you didn't know if she was just growing out of the ground with them. I waited for the float to come near where I stood along the parade route. When it did, I walked out into the street and dropped the ring box among the flowers in front of her."

"What did she do?"

"She opened it and screamed. She looked back at me waving her hand with the ring on it."

"That is so romantic."

"You say it like it's a surprise."

She took a drink of water. "I have no point of reference."

"I guess not," he grunted. "The way we agreed to marry didn't have any of the glow associated with an upcoming marriage."

"It's an in-name-only marriage," Meghan reminded him.

He nodded.

"I do have some questions," she said.

He gestured for her to continue. Meghan waited for the waiter to exchange their salads for entrees. Attentively, he checked to see if they needed anything else, then quietly left them alone.

"I'm a little nobody from Baltimore. I used to be a case worker for a social service organization. You're a businessman, a wizard if I'm to believe the press. Your face has been on national magazines, more than one of which mentioned your eligibility. You travel all over the world. A few moments ago you introduced me to three people and you've nodded to several more. Who are you going to tell these people I am?"

She could see by the blank look on his face that he hadn't thought about it.

"The application for a marriage license is not going to go unnoticed."

"You're right," he said.

"Do you expect me to move into your house and stay sequestered for the next nine months? To be hidden away until the child is delivered?"

"Of course not."

"And then how are you going to explain the baby?" She continued as if he hadn't spoken. "This is what we need to discuss."

"It seems like you've already discussed it," he said. "You want to tell me the outcome?"

Meghan put her fork down and looked him directly in the eye. "I have not done that. While this marriage may not be the forever-and-a-day kind, I wouldn't make any decisions that involve you without discussing them first."

"I stand corrected," he said.

Meghan knew that was as close to an apology as she was likely to get.

"For the record, I do not intend to hide you away for nine months. I'm sure you wouldn't allow it if I tried."

"I need to tell my sister the truth," she said.

"Are you two very close?"

"She's a lot younger, I told you that. We keep in touch. If I change my address to the shore, she's going to ask questions."

"And you'll have to let her know she is not going to be an aunt?"

"That, too."

"Tell her," he said.

He made it sound as if she was a student in the principal's office who'd just gotten out of trouble. Meghan chose to ignore it. She wasn't here for a fight.

"Not what you expected when you invited me to lunch?" She raised her eyebrows.

He smiled as he shook his head.

"I suppose I'm not the type of woman you usually have lunch with."

He stared at her for a long moment. She felt the surge of heat again. Sitting steady under his gaze, she felt his eyes assessing her, as if he could look into her brain and see what she was thinking. Finally, he shook his head.

"I'm used to being able to determine exactly what someone wants. With you…none of the usual rules apply."

Meghan smiled. "I'll take that as a compliment."

"See, not a single woman I know would give me that response."

Meghan's smile widened. "Then I think we should go on." She felt more relaxed, and resumed eating her meal with gusto.

"You're right about other people. What I do will make news. Because you're with me you'll make news, too. They'll want to talk to you."

"And they'll probably ask some pretty probing questions." She rested her chin in her hand and looked at him. "I'm sure you have a PR department that will be willing to coach me."

"Will you take them seriously?"

"Of course," she said, feigning surprise. "Why wouldn't I?"

"I believe you like to shock people. You scrutinize me pretty closely when you say things you think I'm not expecting to hear."

"And it works," she teased. "It's an occupational hazard of being in social work. Sometimes I have to find out what people are really thinking, and not just listen to what they say." Meghan got serious. "Thomas, I would not say anything to the press to embarrass you."

"That's good to know." He looked at her seriously,

too. "I often talk to PR before going on an interview. It helps me keep salient points at the top of my mind. And they can anticipate what you'll be asked."

"I already said I'd go. What about the marriage?"

"Let's keep it to ourselves. The only people who need to know the real reason already know it, except your sister, whom you'll be calling."

She nodded. "Well, that answer makes all the other questions moot."

"There's still background, where we met, how long we've known each other, what's your favorite food, things like that."

They quickly settled on a story that was as true as she could make it. The fact that they had met before eluded Thomas. Meghan didn't take the time to correct him.

Thomas signaled the waiter and settled the bill. He stood, leaving the credit card slip on the table, and helping Meghan up.

"There's only one thing left to do," he said as they stepped from the darkness inside the restaurant into the afternoon light.

"What's that?" she asked.

"We need to get you a ring." He took her arm and led her down the street. "There's a small shop down here that might have exactly the kind of ring to satisfy you."

Meghan walked with him, unsure of what he meant until they turned the corner and she looked up at the imposing sign.

Tiffany & Co.

Chapter 4

It's a small dinner party, Meghan told herself. There was nothing for her to be upset about. She'd already met Thomas's in-laws. It wasn't like she was a real fiancée, meeting the groom's family for the first time and eager for their approval. Then why was she so nervous? She looked at the ring on her left hand. The stone gleamed against the darkness of her finger. She'd thought of something small, or of no engagement ring at all and only a gold wedding band, but Thomas had other ideas and it appeared that Tiffany's didn't sell anything small.

The ring felt heavy on her hand, it also felt strange, unfamiliar. She found it turned on her finger and caught on things. Unconsciously, she would twist it around, glancing at it again and again. What were the people at this dinner party going to think when they saw it? Someone was bound to ask to see the ring.

It was the unknown that made her fidgety. Nina and Adam would be there, which was a consolation. After having spent time with them and listening to them speak about the daughter they had lost, Meaghan had come to respect and like them. But they weren't the only people invited to this small dinner party. Meghan had seen Thomas's house and the formal dining room looked as if it could seat twenty.

She'd shopped for hours for the right dress. Nothing in her closet seemed good enough to grace his table. But she had found something she loved. Evelyn, her neighbor, had come over and done her hair and makeup. Evelyn worked as a hairstylist and was also the neighborhood busybody. But Meghan genuinely liked her. When she'd spied Thomas's car the day he'd come to see Meghan, she'd rushed over as he drove away to dish the dirt. And later when she saw Meghan come in with a dress bag and found out about the dinner party, she'd offered to help Meghan get ready.

Meghan surveyed her reflection in the mirror. She looked great. Evelyn had outdone herself. Meghan's hair was pulled up on top of her head with curls cascading down her back. Her eye shadow was anything but subtle. And while Meghan would have thought the dramatic makeup would only look good on a movie star, she was surprised and pleased at how she looked and felt. Any lingering reservations slid away when Thomas arrived and saw her.

His expression, his in ability to speak for a moment, made it all worth the effort.

"Will I do?" she asked.

He didn't answer. His eyes traveled slowly up from her feet, which were barely covered with strappy high-heeled sandals. The goddess gown was deep violet, made of silk chiffon with a long, full and flowing skirt. The bodice crisscrossed her breasts in glittering sequins and spaghetti straps connected on opposite sides of the low-cut back.

"Thomas," she prompted, his silence beginning to unnerve her.

"Wow," he whispered.

Thomas wore a tuxedo and the contrast of the white shirt against his clean-shaven face was startling. He exuded sex appeal, and dressed as he was, Meghan could melt under the force of it.

She endured his gaze until she felt his eyes were burning through her skin. "Should we go?" she asked.

He stepped forward and lifted her wrap from the sofa where she'd left it. Then he walked around her and placed it on her shoulders. For a moment his hands rested on her arms. Meghan forced herself to breathe.

She was paralyzed, unable to move. Her heart thundered in her chest. This was not good, she told herself. She could not react to Thomas this way. They had a business deal. Nothing more.

"It's a gorgeous dress," he whispered into her ear. "And you look gorgeous in it."

Meghan turned to face him. His breath had been warm on her skin and she'd felt a sizzle all the way down to her toes. She dropped her eyes for a moment before returning her gaze to his deep brown eyes.

"It's a long drive," she said. "We should go." Her voice was soft and low.

Meghan was glad Nina was the first person she saw as she entered the house. "You are beautiful," she said, hugging her.

"Thank you," Meghan replied.

"Just relax and have a good time."

"I will," Meghan said, but she didn't believe it. Through a door only thirty feet away was another world. She didn't know that world, didn't intersect with it at any point. But she was about to walk freely through the door and be an integral part of Thomas Worthington-Yates's life.

Thomas had answered her questions about the dinner guests on the drive there. Meghan took a deep breath and looked back at Thomas. With a smile, he stepped forward and took her wrap, handing it to a maid who appeared quietly out of nowhere.

"Ready?" he whispered.

She smiled even though her heart beat faster. She nodded.

"You'll be fine," he reassured her.

Meghan was thankful that he was on her side. During the drive, she tried to keep her mind off of him. Now she wanted to hold on to him as if he was her anchor.

As they approached the ballroom, the sound grew louder. Meghan heard laughter. It didn't make her feel any better. She hoped she remembered all the details they had discussed on their relationship. She wasn't good at lying, but now it was showtime.

She looked at Thomas just as they reached the doorway. "Stay close," she said. Without thinking, her hand found his. It was warm and strong. She grasped it as if it was a lifeline.

"I'm not throwing you to the wolves," he said. "These are my friends."

"I have the feeling they're going to hate me."

He laughed. "Why?"

"Because I'm not Ruth."

Thomas stopped in mid-stride. He pulled her aside, away from the door. "Meghan Howard. Meghan Howard." He repeated her name. "You will *not* be confused with Ruth."

"It isn't confusion I'm worried about. It's comparison."

"They won't do that."

Meghan rolled her eyes. "They will," she said. "It's human nature. They won't be able to help it."

He looked at his shoes for a second, then back at her. "Can you handle it?"

She nodded, not hesitating for a second. She knew how to appear confident, even if she was shaking inside. And some of her shakes had to do with the man in front of her. A man standing so close she could feel the heat of his body.

Meghan had promised Thomas she would not do anything to embarrass him. After they went in and he got her a drink, he squired her around the room, introducing her to his friends and telling them she was his fiancée.

Meghan scanned their faces for surprise as they shook her hand. In several cases she wasn't disappointed. After the surprise, she felt their smiles were genuine. Some of them were happy for Thomas, even mentioning that it was time for him to move on. Meghan wondered about his relationship with his wife.

After a few moments Meghan felt comfortable enough to move away from Thomas.

"You are a surprise," someone said to her. Meghan turned to find a tall woman with graying hair in front of her. Meghan was good with names. She remembered this woman's name was Olivia Twomley. She and her husband had known Thomas since he was a child. "We didn't even know he was seeing someone."

"We haven't been engaged that long."

"But you've been seeing each other for some time?"

"About a year off and on. Then seriously for the last six months."

"Funny, he didn't mention it."

"He's very busy. Maybe he never got the chance."

She nodded, and Meghan wondered what that meant. Did Olivia believe her or not? Meghan hoped she was convincing.

"Anyway," she said. "Congratulations." She leaned forward and hugged Meghan. "Thomas needs someone in his life. Make him happy."

She left Meghan with a smile. Meghan turned away from the room. She felt like a fraud.

"Are you all right?" Thomas said, immediately coming to her side.

"I'm fine." She turned to him with her smile in place.

"What did Olivia say?"

"She congratulated me."

"You don't sound like she meant it." His tone was guarded.

"I'm sure she did."

"Then what's the problem?"

"No problem."

"Thomas, you ol' fraud," Gary Walls, the president of a local college, joined them with his wife Alice. Gary and Thomas threw soft blows at one another for a moment before they hugged. "You know I would have sworn this man was a confirmed bachelor. And that's despite him being married once." He laughed at his own joke. Meghan smiled as expected.

"That's a beautiful gown," Alice said. She looked at her, admiring the dress. Alice Walls was three sizes larger than Meghan.

"It took me awhile to find it," Meghan said.

At that moment, dinner was announced. Thomas took Meghan's arm and slipped it through his. They had to lead the group into the dining room.

"How's it going?" he asked.

"Better than I expected," she told him. And that was the truth.

"Good night, Meghan. It was a pleasure meeting you."

"Good night, Pepper." Meghan smiled warmly. Pepper took her hand and pulled her into a bear hug. "You're good for him," she whispered before releasing her. "We'll have to get together again soon."

"I'd like that," Meghan replied. Pepper was Fredonia Patterson, a pattern designer for *Vogue Patterns*. She'd complemented Meghan on her dress. She herself wore a simple, straight gown of a clingy pink fabric that flowed like water when she moved.

Adam and Nina were the last to bid them good-
night, Nina with a twinkle in her eye and a wide smile
on her face.

"I had a wonderful time," Nina told her. She pressed
her cheek first to Meghan's and then to Thomas's. Adam
did the same and the two went to a waiting car.

Thomas held the door open, his arm around
Meghan's waist, until the driver closed the door and
Nina and Adam disappeared from sight. As the driver
turned out of the circular driveway, Thomas closed the
door and turned to her.

"Tired?"

She shook her head. "I should be. Especially because
I was so nervous. Do you think they bought it?" Meghan
wasn't used to deception. She needed complete honesty
from the clients she dealt with in Social Services. And
she needed to be completely honest with them. Many
of their problems stemmed from deception and dishon-
esty. She hadn't been completely comfortable with deceiving Thomas's friends, some of whom she liked, but
there was no way around it if Thomas wanted to save
his reputation and keep the press at bay. And Meghan
didn't want to defend her position as a surrogate.

"I think you were magnificent. Even Olivia seemed
to warm to you."

"I'm not so sure about her."

Thomas put his hand on her lower back and guided
her toward the living room. He'd done that a lot during
the evening. Meghan felt jumpy each time she felt it, but
hoped no one noticed. She knew he was being reassuring, that he was letting her know he was there for her,

ready to deflect any untoward comments. None had been delivered. For the most part, his friends were accepting.

Meghan had felt Thomas was still in love with his wife. Tonight she discovered he had yet to complete the grieving process. She saw it in the smiles of his friends, in their willingness to believe that he had at last found love again. The knowledge depressed her. Thomas's "new relationship" was a facade, only the image of what they expected.

Meghan glanced at the dining room which had been completely cleared by the catering staff, though music was still playing from a stereo system that was out of sight. Meghan hummed along with the song, unsure what was going on now. They should be getting her wrap and going to the car for the long drive back into the city. Instead a maid came silently into the room and placed a tray of fruit, cheese and two champagne glasses on the coffee table. She smiled and left as quietly as she had entered.

Thomas lifted the two flutes that had already been filled, and handed one to her.

"What shall we drink to?" she asked. "Since this is likely my last drink for the next nine months."

"New beginnings," he said after a moment.

Meghan nodded and clinked her glass against his. She drank the champagne. It was sparkly and tickled her nose. Thomas popped a square of cheese into his mouth. Meghan selected and ate some grapes. They were exquisitely sweet and balanced the wine.

She glanced at Thomas. He was quiet. The kind of silence that meant he was thinking of something, reviewing, remembering other times, other events, another woman. A wave of jealously went through Meghan. She mentally shook herself, knowing she had no right to those feelings.

"You said you thought I did well tonight."

He looked at her. The two lines between his brows deepened.

"How did you do?"

"What?"

"From something someone said, this is the first time you've had a dinner party and invited someone you were *interested* in to meet your friends." Nina had told her that. Meghan purposely didn't say who had given her the information. "So, are you all right?"

He stood up and walked to the unlit fireplace. "I wouldn't tell anyone else this," he began.

Meghan knew they were not intimate and not likely to be. But she also knew more about him than he often allowed other people to see.

"It wasn't easy tonight. I kept remembering…"

"Other parties…Ruth," she supplied when he trailed off.

"I know it's morbid, but it was impossible not to comp—not to remember seeing all our friends."

"Thomas, are you sure you want to do this? You can back out. I won't hold it against you. If you're not ready, I'll understand."

He was shaking his head before she finished her comment.

"Then are you doing it for the right reason?"

"The right reason?" His brow crinkled again. Meghan

wanted to reach up and smooth it out. She was glad she was still seated.

"Because you want to be a father. Because you want to love and rear a child? Or are you doing it because you think it's what Ruth would want you to do?"

"Is there something wrong in my wanting to have a child with the woman I loved?"

"Nothing at all," Meghan stated. "Children should be created out of love. And I have no doubt that you loved your wife. I believe you still love her."

"So a child is the natural progression."

"Progression of a relationship. Of a family. That avenue has been cut short for you. So the natural progression is to move on."

"That is not an option for me." His voice said his comment was not open to further discussion.

"You have an option to go a step further, and I am a willing participant to fulfill that option. But I've seen the effects on the children of parents who miscalculate the changes required of them for family. Being a single father with your business and the necessity to travel forces me to ask if you've truly thought through all the changes you'll have to make for this child."

"No, I haven't," he said.

Meghan did not expect him to admit it.

"Then are you rethinking the agreement?"

"No," he answered again. "I believe it's impossible to completely understand what will be necessary before it really happens. I've observed other people with their children, but without a twenty-four-seven, long-term period with children, it's not possible to know. But I'm willing to make the effort, to do what is necessary for this child."

He said it as if there was already a child. Meghan took another drink from her flute. The champagne no longer tasted as good.

She stood up and joined him. "You're a very honest man," she said. "I think you'll make a good father."

"Was that an interview?" he asked. "Were you testing me, practicing your craft as a social worker to see if I'm fit to raise a child?" His voice was edged with anger.

"Yes," she said succinctly. "And you passed."

Chapter 5

If the procedure worked, Thomas and Meghan were going to spend nine months together. He wondered if she would continue to catch him off guard and render him speechless the way she had just done.

"Are there to be more of these tests in the future?"

"I don't think so. Your heart's in the right place. I believe you truly want a baby and that you're willing to do what it takes to provide love, comfort and a home for him or her."

"That sounds like a report you'd give the court."

"You've already been before the court. You have Nina and Adam as a support system, and I've already said you passed. Now I should be getting home."

He didn't want her to go. She looked great in that dress. Thomas wondered what she'd look like out of it.

He'd seen the way other men stared at her, some even commenting on how lucky he was.

"Should I find the maid and get my wrap?" she asked.

"It's in the hall closet. I'll get the car," he said, moving past her.

"You're not going to drive me?"

He stopped and turned back. "Sure I am."

"You have to be tired. You drove all the way in to pick me up. If you drive me back and then come home, that's a three-hour turnaround." She glanced at the clock on the mantle. "You won't get home until daylight. I assumed a car service would drive me back. Or Nina and Adam's driver."

"Don't worry about the drive. I do it regularly. And I'm staying the night in the city."

Moments later, the two were ensconced in the interior of the same sedan he'd picked her up in. Thomas drove in silence for several minutes. Meghan had said she wasn't tired, but her body sagged against the upholstery. The dinner was an ordeal for her. He knew it, but she'd won over his friends. The approved whispers and promises to see her again let him know that they'd accepted her.

Had she won him over as well? Thomas wondered.

When he'd seen her in that gown in her living room, he wanted to skip his own party and spend the evening whispering in her ear. For a moment, he thought she had the same idea.

Glancing at her, Thomas noticed Meghan had fallen asleep. She was beautiful even with her eyes closed. The drive took over an hour, but it felt like only minutes.

She was affecting him as no other woman, except Ruth, had done.

Parking in front of her house, he cut the engine and turned to face her. She didn't stir. Thomas released her seat belt and removed it without disturbing her. Then he went around to the passenger side and opened the door, hunkering down to her level.

"Meghan," he whispered. She opened her eyes, but they didn't focus. She closed them again. "Meghan, you're home."

She opened her eyes, blinking several times, looking around to orient herself.

"Did I sleep all the way?"

"Afraid you did."

"I'm so sorry," she said, yawning. "It was rude of me."

"I didn't consider it rude," he said.

Twisting her body, she put her feet on the ground and leaned forward. Thomas helped her stand up. Once she was standing, he didn't relinquish his hold on her, but kept his arm around her waist.

He'd done that throughout the night, giving the impression that he was being affectionate. It wasn't a stretch. And he'd gotten used to the feel of her.

She found her keys in the small beaded bag she carried and opened her door. Then she turned to him.

"It was a nice party," she said. "You have wonderful friends and they care about you. Thanks for introducing me."

"You did all the work. I should thank you."

For a moment they said nothing. The air between them changed, electrified. He became aware of himself, of the way his hand was holding hers, the small amount of space that separated them. He felt like a teenager again, saying good-night to his first date and wondering whether it was appropriate to kiss her.

With Meghan he knew it wasn't, but that didn't stop him from wanting to feel the softness of her mouth, taste the sweetness of her being. Feel her body pressed against his.

Then she took matters into her own hands. Standing on her toes, she kissed his cheek. Without knowing it, Thomas's hands caught her waist and held her in place. She moved her head back to look at him. Their mouths were only a kiss apart. Thomas felt her breath. He was mesmerized by it. He looked into her eyes—eyes that drew him to her as if she was some exotic goddess.

"What was that for?" Thomas thought he should say something, move away and break the connection that was holding them together, but he ignored all warning signs. He hadn't felt like this in a long while and he liked it.

"Familiarity. If I'm to play a role, I don't want to be surprised by it."

He knew she meant his arm around her waist. The first time he'd touched her, he could feel the surprise pass through her, but she'd relaxed as he'd touched her more often. But he was thinking of touching her now and it had nothing to do with their agreement. He wanted to feel her, all of her.

He wasn't sure if Meghan moved toward him or shifted in place, but the result was the same. His mouth covered hers. His arms tightened around her waist and he aligned his body with hers. She was soft and curved in all the right places. She fit into him as if the two had been made for each other.

Thomas slipped his tongue into her mouth, tasting the nectar he had thought about since first seeing her this afternoon. Their mouths melded, tongues danced. Her arms snaked around his neck as she joined him in full measure. He kissed her with desperation, holding her tight, pushing his hands into her hair and searing her mouth with his.

It had been a long, long time. And suddenly, he wanted her, wanted all of her. His hands roamed along her back and over her hips. Heat poured into him and pooled in his growing erection. Thomas took control of himself. Gently, he pushed her back.

"Good night," he said.

"Good morning," she answered with a sly smile. After a short hesitation, she stepped inside and closed the door.

Thomas let out a long breath and hung his head.

What the hell was he thinking?

Meghan's sneakers made that squishy sound that rubber soles did against concrete. Her feet pounded the pavement. Her grunts punctuated the air in rhythmic syncopation with her steps. She kept waiting for the endorphin trigger to kick in, that feel-good place where her mind would clear and she would feel as calm and happy as if she had no worries.

This morning it didn't seem to be working. Her mind and her body knew something was different. And that was blocking everything else. Like she often told clients, they needed to face their issues to resolve them. And here she was trying to avoid hers. Trying to head off thoughts of Thomas and the way he'd kissed her. The way she had responded. And worse, the way she wanted to see him again and have him kiss her in the same way he had done on her doorstep.

Meghan topped the hill at Columbus Avenue. Usually at this point, she'd reached the top of her jogging circle and would begin her return. But her mind continued to be active. Without thought, her feet pressed on, veering away from the circle.

She pressed forward, continuing, not thinking about her route, but unable to force her thoughts off Thomas Worthington-Yates and his arms embracing her, her body pressed to his hard muscular frame.

She looked up at the sky as she kept going. She felt her legs. Her calves ached. Looking around, Meghan recognized the landmarks. Ahead of her was Lincoln Park. She was two miles farther than her longest run. Five miles from home.

Meghan slowed her momentum and by the time she reached the paved circular path in the park, her energy level was down to a walk. But she felt like crawling. She wanted to drop to the grass and fall face-first onto the ground. Sweat poured off her golden brown skin. Her hair, which she'd pulled into a ponytail and knotted on top of her head, had fallen down. Wet tendrils adhered to her neck and shoulders. Her mouth was parched. Her legs burned from overdoing it and she must've been taking in three times as much oxygen as normal if the rise and fall of her chest was any indication.

Seeing a juice bar set up on the edge of the track and umbrella tables with seating, she headed toward them, wondering if her legs would carry her the ten yards. Buying an expensive bottle of cranberry juice, she dropped into a seat closest to the track.

She took a long swallow of the juice, being careful not to drink too much or too fast.

Meghan felt her energy level rising. She needed to rest a little longer before returning home. Two miles out of her usual routine meant it would take her a lot longer to get home if she didn't call someone. She'd already rejected taking any kind of public transportation due to her personal hygiene needs.

Evelyn Garrison was home, Meghan thought. Her neighbor would come and get her. Of course, Evelyn would complain about the state of Meghan's hair and her lack of makeup. She'd reached for the zippered pocket on her shorts for her cell phone, when her fingers suddenly went numb.

It couldn't be, she told herself. She blinked. Then squinted. Her eyes closed and opened. Nothing changed. The vision continued, getting closer and closer with each jogging step. The apparition she didn't want to see, clarified until she couldn't deny the identity of the man about to come face to face with her. Unconsciously, Meghan twisted the ring on her finger.

Thomas hadn't seen her yet, hadn't connected his gaze to crystallize her features into the unique individual she was. Meghan didn't want to see him. He'd disturbed every cell in her body, and she wanted more time before she had to confront both him and her feelings. At this moment they were both jumbled and confused.

She couldn't leave, couldn't move or she'd draw attention to herself. She had no hat to pull down to camouflage her features. She must look like hell. Meghan prayed he'd be so far in the zone that he wouldn't notice her. She told herself there must be hundreds of women who jogged here, hundreds who sat at these tables and drank juice. Why should he notice her?

She stared, keeping her body rigid, and her eyes trained on a single point in space. But it was no use. She couldn't keep her eyes off him. Her head moved with his movements, taking in the glistening sheen on his muscular frame. He was gorgeous, wearing only shorts and shoes. Meghan took in the length of his legs, the way his muscles contracted and expanded as he ran. She studied each section of his body individually, long legs and thighs, a tapered waist that held a torso that looked like it had been carved by Michelangelo's chisel. Broad shoulders ended in corded arms. And the entire package was covered with flawless skin. Meghan couldn't keep the parts of him segmented. Her mind melded them, putting him together into a single, moving machine of muscle and bone that had Meghan panting.

Her heartbeat pounded and the cooling her body had accomplished previously was completely lost in the heat of his presence.

And then he saw her.

Surprise widened his deep brown eyes and they connected with hers. He stopped his run. Meghan thought he stumbled, but he recovered so quickly she was sure she'd imagined it.

Leaning forward with his hands on his knees, he sucked in air. Seeing Meghan had jolted him out of the zone. His body was reacting to the sudden reduction of endorphins, the stoppage of muscle movement. The machinery had been shut down, not slowed and allowed to cool in the normal manner.

Standing up, Thomas jumped in place, rapidly bending each knee. Then he stopped and stretched his legs, pulling each knee up to his chest, then bending each one behind him to keep his body from cramping. Meghan sat like a boulder, unable to move, but capable of riotous feelings, all of which ripped through her.

Thomas came forward and dropped into the chair opposite her. "I didn't know you ran," he said, looking at her clothes. Meghan was dressed for jogging. She'd been doing it as an alternative to joining a gym.

"With all the rich meals I've had in the past few weeks, I need to do something to counteract weight gain."

She'd tried for levity, but Thomas's expression didn't change.

"I've never seen you here before." He used his arm to wipe away sweat that poured from his face. Meghan reached into her zippered pocket and handed him a clean shammy along with the remainder of her drink.

"I don't usually jog here. I prefer the streets."

He drained the bottle and dried his face, arms and chest. Meghan couldn't stop herself from following the path of the shammy cloth as it mapped his body. Meghan had the insane thought of taking the cloth and rubbing it all over his body. Again heat assailed her.

"Why?" he asked.

It took her a moment to understand his question. "I like to see things," she said. "The streets have buildings, people, the land isn't uniform. It has inclines and depressions—things to make the run interesting."

"But that may not be the best place to run."

She knew he made reference to the area where she lived. "No better, no worse than here. And I'm careful. I know most of the people on my normal route. Today I went a little farther."

He stared directly in her eyes. "You jogged here?" His eyebrows went up. "From your house?"

She nodded. Her throat closed off and she felt like a child being caught doing something wrong. "I'm not planning to jog back. I was about to call a friend to come and pick me up."

Thomas stood up. "Come on. I'll drive you home."

"That's not necessary."

"Can you stand up?" he asked.

"Of course I can stand up," she answered, but made no move to prove it.

"Are your legs burning?"

"No." She lied for no reason. Why shouldn't she tell him she'd run too far and that the nitrogen had collected in her leg muscles?

"Good," he said. "Stand up."

He reached for her hand. Meghan hesitated a moment. Not because she couldn't stand, but because she was unsure how she'd react to his touch.

Slipping her hand into his, she felt his soft palm. Doctor's hand, she thought. She tried to view him in that capacity, as a doctor, someone impartial and without prejudice.

It didn't work.

Meghan stood up, locking her knees and keeping herself erect.

Evelyn Garrison was descending the stairs when Thomas parked his car in front of Meghan's house. A smile showed her gleaming, white teeth as Thomas got out of the car and came around to help Meghan. Thomas had put on a T-shirt, but he still wore the shorts that hugged his tight butt so well Meghan wanted to cup the buns in her hands.

She didn't miss the smile on Evelyn's face as she casually waved and pulled the door to her car open.

"I can't wait to get into the shower," Meghan said.

"Do you mind if I shower, too?" Thomas asked.

Lights burst so brightly through her mind that she grabbed onto the car to wait for the blindness to subside. Unfortunately when it did, she had a mental image of the two of them naked in her shower.

"I have a meeting downtown and if I go to my office, I'll be late for it."

Meghan tried to understand his words, but her mind was elsewhere.

"What did you say?"

"I have a meeting I need to get to and I want to use your shower."

"Sure," she said. "Sure."

Thomas pulled a change of clothes from the trunk of his car and together they went into the house. It always felt small when he was there.

The house had only one shower and it was in the

en suite off the bedroom. At this moment Meghan wished she'd installed the shower Suzanne had always wanted in the second bathroom.

"The shower is in the first room on the left at the top of the stairs." Thomas immediately raced up the stairs, taking them two at a time and finding the bedroom as if he had been there several times.

Meghan let out a long breath when she heard the bathroom door close. She sat down, then thought of Thomas removing his clothes and standing under the spray of water. On the jogging track, he wore only shorts and shoes. Meghan had studied his features as if she were an art student. The truth was, she couldn't tear her gaze away. She could imagine him now, his body wet and naked. Never had she wanted to touch a man, run her hands over him the way she wanted to rush up the steps and join Thomas in her shower. Meghan had to stop. She opened her mouth and panted, shaking her hands in the air, trying to cool the heat her thoughts had created.

Catching a glance of herself in the microwave, she noted her reflection was disheveled and unattractive. She nearly jumped off the chair. Sprinting up the stairs, she rushed into Suzanne's bathroom. She'd never moved so fast. Turning on the taps, she stripped and knelt in the tub, sluicing water all over herself and quickly bathing with a sponge.

She had to work fast. She needed to get into her bedroom and get clothes on before Thomas came out of the shower. She didn't want him to catch her wrapped in only the fluffy white towel she'd curled around herself.

And she knew, as much as she imagined him in the buff, he didn't want to be surprised by her unexpected presence when he opened that door.

Pulling a sundress over her still-damp body, Meghan tucked her hair into a scrunchy. Pushing her feet into low-heeled sandals, she settled for lipstick, eye shadow and a light powder to enhance her cheeks.

Returning to the kitchen, she put on a pot of coffee and then opened the refrigerator. It was stocked with food. Meghan didn't eat out often. She'd carried her lunch to work, often the remainders of the previous night's dinner. She wasn't a go-to-the-mall-and-eat-while-you-shop person. If she got hungry, her first thought was to go home.

Now she stood in front of enough food to feed several families and she couldn't decide if she should cook something or not. She hadn't eaten before going out and now she wasn't sure she could get anything to pass her throat. Thomas was still upstairs. She listened for him moving around, but the house had been built solidly and she could hear nothing.

She reached for the eggs, not thinking why she wanted them. The coffeepot gurgled.

"Coffee," she said out loud, as if it could save her.

"I'll have a cup."

Startled, Meghan turned and nearly dropped the eggs.

"Wow!" Thomas said.

"Wow!" Meghan said at the same time. Thomas looked good enough to eat. And at this moment, she just might take a bite out of him.

"While I was in the shower, I was thinking," he said.

Meghan handed him a cup of coffee and offered him sugar and cream. He passed on both.

"What were you thinking?"

"I was thinking about a play."

"Are you an actor now?"

He laughed at her joke, shaking his head. "Would you like to go tonight?"

"To see what?"

He shook his head. "Whatever is playing at the national theater."

"In D.C.?"

"We could go to Broadway, but that would take longer and we'd miss the opening."

Meghan knew he was teasing her. She wasn't used to his world, a place where people picked up and did what they wanted with no thought to the cost of it.

"Are you entertaining business clients?"

"No clients. Just us."

Meghan forced herself not to smile. She kept her face straight, although her heart was screaming for joy. "Just us?" She needed confirmation.

He nodded. "Don't you like the theater?"

"I love it."

"Good. I'll pick you up at six-thirty."

He set his cup down and with a nod headed for the door with his gym bag in tow. Meghan followed him. At the front door she called his name and he turned to her.

"You don't have to do this," she told him.

"Do what?"

"You don't have to take me out. I mean alone. If you have clients to woo or you need to convince people our relationship is normal, I'll support your needs. I've already agreed to the surrogacy. I won't back out."

Thomas set his gym bag down and straightened up. "Did it ever occur to you that I might want to be alone with you?"

Meghan shook her head.

"Well, let me remind you."

He took a step toward her, cupped her face in his hands and aimed for her mouth. Meghan turned her head and his lips landed on her side of her mouth.

Refusing his kiss was the hardest thing she'd ever done. She still felt waves of sensation coursing through her at just the tiniest of touches from him. She wanted the full-blown sensual waltz. She wanted him to sweep her off her feet, carry her back into the house, and make passionate love to her. But they didn't have that kind of relationship. He was from the clean, uniformed lines on a running-track world and she was the zigzag-over-cracked-sidewalks type. Eventually, they would both return to their separate worlds.

"Don't do that again," she said when he pushed back. "We both need to remember what we're doing."

Thomas took a step back. It was one step, but Meghan knew the gulf between them stretched the length of the Baltimore Beltway.

"I apologize," he said. They stared at each other. Meghan didn't know what to say or do. The air between them hissed with tension. Meghan was close enough to see Thomas's jaw tighten.

"Don't misunderstand me," she said. "I'm a realist

and when this is all over, I want to be able to walk away with my emotions intact."

"And I'm a threat to those emotions."

She looked down, then back up. "I think you know you are."

Meghan didn't know what she expected him to say or even if she expected him to say anything. He didn't speak, but he also didn't drop his gaze. Like fighters facing off and ready to battle, the two of them stood their ground.

"You're right," he said.

Meghan wasn't sure what he was agreeing with her on. The fact that he knew he tested her emotions, or that they would part in nine months.

"You're right," he said again. "I suppose I was forgetting the arrangement. I promise it won't happen again."

He retrieved his bag from the floor and faced her again. "I'll leave the two tickets at the box office. You can use them or not. I don't care."

Chapter 6

"Ladies, gentlemen, thank you." Thomas watched the meeting break up. The investors he employed filed out of the conference room to return to their duties—the business of making money. Thomas owned a small investment house. He was doing well. Even in this economy, Thomas was holding his own. He had a good staff, one that needed expanding if their predictions were true. And he had no reason to doubt them. He wished his thoughts on Meghan would coalesce into something as identifiable as the market.

He sat down in the big leather chair and slumped back against the butter-soft upholstery. The long conference table stretched out before him. Thomas was thinking of Meghan and their encounter that morning.

Just seeing her had kicked his heart rate up a couple of notches.

He didn't know she jogged. There were so many things he didn't know about her. When he took her home, showered in her bathroom, he thought it might be good to get to know more about her, but she'd crushed that thought.

And rightfully so.

Thomas might be getting married again, but he never planned to get emotionally involved with another woman. Somehow he was forgetting that with Meghan, but she'd reminded him of it this morning. He should have thanked her. Instead he threw her reminder in her face.

And he couldn't get her out of his mind. The way her hair fell to the nape of her neck. After his shower, when he'd found her in her kitchen, her back to him, looking into the refrigerator, that space at the back of her neck was exposed. Calling to him. Begging him to cover the small space of skin with his kiss.

Thank heaven he hadn't acted on the thought.

Getting up, he returned to his office. The desk was covered with paper. He didn't sit down, but stood next to his chair and looked at the photo of Ruth on his desk. He'd carried her in his heart for a long while, given her a place of honor in his life. *How could he so easily forget that when he was with Meghan?*

Their relationship was temporary. Nine short months. Then she'd be gone and he'd have the child he and Ruth had wanted. Meghan would be a memory. There was no need to get involved in her life, no need to learn her likes and dislikes. No need to think about sitting in a dark theater with her, watching her as she saw the actors on the stage. No need to think of laughing with her, or having that late supper.

Thomas took a deep breath. He grabbed the computer mouse and looked at the screen. It was time to work. Meghan had to go to the back of his mind.

Damn, he cursed. The tickets.

He reached for the phone, but it buzzed indicating his secretary was calling him. Punching the button, he spoke into the air.

"Yes."

"If you don't leave now, you're going to be late for lunch."

"I'm on my way," Thomas said. He went to punch the release button, when he remembered the tickets. "Rhonda, would you call the National and order two tickets for tonight's performance? Have them left at Will Call under the name of Meghan Howard?"

"Certainly," she said.

Thomas took a moment to get the mental images that dropped into his head each time he thought of Meghan in order before leaving for his appointment. He didn't see the anger that was on her face at his last words. He saw the soft-looking woman in the yellow sundress, who'd aroused him.

Pushing that image away, Thomas stood up and pushed his arms into the suit jacket that was hanging behind the door. He adjusted his tie and left his office. As he passed his secretary, the phone rang. Thomas shook his head and continued toward the elevator.

The restaurant wasn't that far away, but he couldn't

walk there. The day was hot, much hotter than it had been when he was jogging. He considered removing the jacket, but decided against it. Jumping into a taxi, he knew it would take a while to get to *La Marseilles* in the downtown traffic.

Thomas spent the time thinking about Meghan. She slipped into his mind, like a fond memory. This morning when he'd come across her sitting in the park, his body had lurched, but he'd managed not to let his step falter. He was sorry he'd left her angry. He wanted to kiss her and she'd rejected him.

The taxi stopped. Thomas checked his watch. He'd lost track of time, but he was a few minutes early for the meeting. Getting out of the cab, his hand instinctively went to his hip where he kept his wallet. The space was devoid of the bulge he expected to find there. That sinking feeling dropped his stomach to the ground. Pulling the back door open again, he checked the seat to see if it had fallen out of his pocket, although he knew that was nearly impossible with the depth of the pocket.

Thomas didn't know what he was going to do. He'd need to call his secretary and have her come over and bail him out. He reached for his cell phone.

Behind him someone came up. He was sure they wanted the taxi.

"I think this is what you're looking for." Thomas turned to find Meghan behind him. She was holding his wallet. "I called because I found your wallet on the floor in my bedroom."

He took it and paid the driver.

"I called your office, but you'd already left. Your

secretary only gave me your location when I told her I was your fiancée."

"Thank you," he said. "This is a very important meeting."

"What kind of meeting is it?" Meghan said.

"It's a new client. If I close the deal, we'll control a portfolio worth millions. It has a potential to grow into serious money after that."

"I suppose I should go so you can prepare for it. Good luck." She turned and walked away.

Thomas stopped her after three steps. She was no longer wearing the yellow sundress, but had changed into a white short-sleeve suit. Her hair looked like it did last night, with scores of curls cascading down from a grouping at the top of her head. He wanted to bury his hands in that hair and watch it fall about her neck and shoulders, but he remembered what had happened that morning.

"About this morning," he said when he reached her.

"Don't," she said, raising her hands to ward off any apology.

"You were right," Thomas stated. "I forgot our agreement. It won't happen again. I understand your motives for being a surrogate and I won't infringe on them again."

"In the long run, it's for the best," she said.

He nodded.

Another taxi pulled up in front of the restaurant. Two men and two women got out. They looked up and down the street and then settled their attention on the two of them.

"Is that your party?"

"They're right on time," Thomas answered.

"Do they know I'm your fiancée?"

"Probably not you specifically, but they know I'm engaged."

"Then you'd better kiss me goodbye."

It was the last thing Thomas expected her to say. They were on a public street. When they stood in her doorway, she'd refused him, but in front of an audience it was all right. Maybe she thought it was controllable. It hadn't been last night, Thomas thought. Street or no street, he didn't trust himself to touch her lips. They were full and sexy, the most kissable lips he'd noticed in longer than he cared to admit.

Thomas leaned forward and kissed her cheek. He held her a little longer than was necessary. Her hands clasped his arms and she whispered, "Good luck."

Pushing away from him, she adjusted her suit. "You look like you're on your way somewhere." He wondered if she thought he'd invite her to lunch. He could. He'd like to.

"I have an appointment."

The way she said it made it seem as if she left something out.

"With whom?" he'd asked before he thought better of it.

"Dr. Rayford Armstrong at the Newburg Fertility Center for a consultation."

She couldn't have knocked the wind out of him more successfully if she'd told him she was already pregnant.

Thomas stood for a long time watching her walk away. She held her head high and walked like a model. She didn't look back.

* * *

Thomas didn't remember the tickets he'd left for Meghan until he was sitting in front of her house, several hours after she'd left him on the street. He'd wanted to hear the results of her visit to the center, but when he knocked on her door there had been no answer. Apparently, she'd gone to the theater for the evening. He had always accompanied Ruth to the procedures. Thomas felt she needed his support at this time. Meghan wasn't doing this under the same circumstances as his wife had, but Thomas thought he should support her as well.

Thomas drove back to his apartment. Once there, he called Nina and Adam. He hadn't checked in with them in a couple of days.

"Have you talked to Meghan?" he asked after greeting them.

"This morning, after you left for the office." They knew he'd been at Meghan's this morning. It felt like days ago.

"Did you know she was going to the clinic today?"

"We offered to go with her, but she said she wanted to do it alone."

Why didn't she tell me? he said to himself.

"Where is she now?" Nina asked.

"As far as I know, she went to the theater." He didn't tell Nina that he was the one who supplied the tickets. Or that she was in the District, fifty miles away. He had no idea who she went with.

"Why don't you call her cell phone if you're concerned?" Adam spoke.

He looked at his watch. "The play has probably already started."

"Give her a call after it's over."

"Maybe I will."

They dropped the subject of Meghan and after several more minutes of small talk, Thomas hung up.

He walked about rooms he was familiar with, but looked at them as if he was renewing his acquaintance with them. Ruth had always come home from the procedure and gone to bed. Afterward, she'd taken it easy for a full day just to make sure. Meghan had gone into the District to attend a play.

Thomas wasn't sure if he should be glad or angry. He was nervous. Had the procedure worked? Thomas had asked himself that question several times as he watched the hours tick by.

When his cell phone rang, for a moment he didn't know what the sound was. He was surprised to find Meghan's name on the display screen of his phone.

He answered.

"Nina called to say you were looking for me."

Dear Nina, he thought. *One of these days I'm going to strangle her.* "I wanted to discuss the procedure. We didn't think you would go through it alone."

"Thomas, you misunderstood." She didn't elaborate and he thought she might not be alone. "I'll explain it all to you later."

He realized it now. She couldn't have gone through a procedure. She had a consultation. In order to complete the procedure, she'd have to have all the papers signed and everything in place. They'd signed nothing thus far.

Thomas sighed heavily, letting out the breath he was

holding in. He'd forgotten the steps necessary to go through an implantation. When it happened for real, he planned to be there.

"How was the play?" he asked, searching for something else to say.

"Great, funny, not to be missed," she teased.

Thomas heard noise in the background. She was in her car. He could hear the wind outside as she drove.

"Are you on your way home now?"

"Yes," she said. "In fact, I'm just passing your apartment. Evelyn and I are almost home."

"Evelyn?" So she wasn't alone.

"She's my neighbor and friend." Thomas heard a muffled voice in the background. "Evelyn says thank-you for the ticket. She enjoyed the play."

"My pleasure," he answered, relieved that Meghan had chosen a female friend to go with her. Why it should matter, he wondered, but refused to think about at this moment.

"How was your meeting? Did it go well?"

"It did. I got the contract."

"Great." She sounded happy for him. "You'll have to go out and celebrate."

The thought hadn't occurred to him. The people at his office were glad when he returned to give them the news. The legal department would follow up and get all the details signed and sealed. He'd been more interested in Meghan and what she was doing. When they left that night, Thomas had pleaded exhaustion. Instead of going home, he'd driven straight to Meghan's house, only to find her gone.

"I need to talk to you soon."

He wanted to be there for her.

"How about tomorrow?"

"At the jogging track?" she suggested.

"I'll pick you up. We can drive there together. And I'll spring for the juice."

Thomas's silver sedan was becoming a familiar sight in front of Meghan's house. She was waiting for him when he arrived early the next morning. For a moment Meghan peeked through the window. She loved looking at him. He wore shorts and a T-shirt with no sleeves that stopped at his midriff. His bare arms and legs were strong and powerfully built.

As he headed for the door, Meghan pulled it open and walked out. She stepped onto the porch, wearing blue jogging shorts and a top that was little more than a jogging bra.

"Ready?" he asked. Meghan noticed him admiring the amount of skin she was showing, but he said nothing and made no attempt to touch her.

"I'm ready."

They walked down the steps. "Do you have a change of clothes in there?" she asked.

He glanced at the car. A lazy smile curved his mouth. "Do you mind?"

She shook her head. "I have an idea, though."

"What?"

"Instead of us going to the park, why don't we go on my route?"

"Through the streets?"

She nodded.

He put his arm out in a gesture for her to precede him. "When in Rome."

Meghan started her run. Baltimore was a city of contrasts. Some streets ended at the harbor. Anything from small inclines to steep hills could be found. The route Meghan took was an ever-changing path of concrete. She started out at a fast pace. Thomas matched her.

"Am I slowing you down?"

"This is a good pace," he said.

She didn't usually talk when she jogged. Jogging was a solitary sport. It was an exercise for the mind and the body. It was to calm the mind, free it to work on problems while the body was awake, instead of doing the job only when the conscious brain slept.

There was a routine to her workout. It didn't involve stretching, or warm-ups, although she never began a run without doing those things. This routine was waving and smiling at the people along her route. While she didn't come down the same streets at the same time every day, she did see the same people often.

"Hello Ms. Shaw." Meghan waved to a white-haired lady sitting in a window on the second floor. She smiled and waved back. Glancing at Thomas, she explained, "She can't walk, but her mind is sharp."

They ran another block. Up ahead, Mr. Gonzalez came out of his market. In front of it were baskets turned on their sides, spilling fruits and vegetables like a horn of plenty. He saw her and immediately ducked inside the store.

"Someone who doesn't like you?" Thomas asked.

"Just wait," she said.

As they reached the store, he stepped out and held out two bottles of water.

"Thank you," Meghan shouted, taking them and continuing her run. She handed one to Thomas, who laughed at the choreographed way she and Mr. Gonzalez worked. "When I first met him, he slipped me one of those huge cupcakes with heaps of icing on top for Suzanne. After I started jogging this way, he'd come out and pass me a bottle of water." Meghan didn't tell him that three days after she discovered the cupcake, she had returned and paid for it. And she would pay him for the water the next time she shopped in his store.

Together they ran, keeping pace with each other. Meghan smiled and acknowledged more people along the route. She pointed out some of the buildings, giving Thomas a little history of the area. By the time they got back to her house, he was breathing hard.

"Did I go too fast?" she asked.

"No…no," he said, puffing.

Meghan smiled. "Understand what I mean about the streets?"

"Oh, yeah," he said.

"Come on in. I'll get you a glass of water." They'd finished the bottles Mr. Gonzalez had given them halfway through the course.

"I brought the juice," Thomas said between breaths.

Meghan laughed at his obvious discomfort. "Maybe you'd better bring it in. If you can walk," she added.

"And I thought I was in great shape."

Meghan wasn't about to touch that. She couldn't help but stare at him, though. Despite his comment, he moved easily. Her eyes followed him as if they were hungry for sight. His shirt was wet, plastered to his back, outlining the contours of the skin beneath it. Meghan forced herself to turn away before she got to the length of his legs, the sheen of sweat that turned his skin golden brown, the hard muscles that bunched and relaxed as he walked.

She opened the door, not waiting for him to get his bag. Inside she did her cool-down routine, but it wasn't working today. Getting a glass of water, she drank deeply.

"You run that route every day?" Thomas said, coming into the house and dropping his bag in the center of the room. He followed her into the kitchen, carrying a small cooler.

"Not always. Sometimes I take different routes."

"And you appear to know everyone you passed."

"It's a friendly neighborhood. Isn't your neighborhood friendly?"

"I don't know. I never jog though my neighborhood."

"Isn't it considered…proper?" She used her hands to put air quote marks around the word proper.

"No, it's just that there are places we go to jog."

Opening the cooler, Thomas removed two bottles of orange juice. He offered her one. Meghan took it. Grabbing a towel, she dried the slushy ice and the water dripping from it. Thomas stood gulping his down, water trickling onto her floor.

Meghan wanted to laugh. He might live in a community where a weed was dead meat, but here he was plain folk.

And she liked that.

Chapter 7

An hour later they were still sitting in her kitchen. Meghan had made a light breakfast and the two of them ate it at her kitchen table. Thomas had her laughing over stories of his childhood and horror stories of him expanding his business. His father had given him a challenge and he'd turned that challenge into the business he now ran.

"Speaking of business," she said. "Don't you have a job to get to?"

"Is that your way of telling me I've overstayed my welcome?"

"Not at all. But you do have a business to run," she said.

"I took the morning off."

"You did?" Meghan wondered why. She got the impression that he didn't often take days off. He was the type who worked no matter what. Had he done it to spend time with her?

"I wanted to hear about yesterday."

"What about yesterday?"

"Your consultation. You didn't go to the same place where Ruth and I went."

"I had some questions. I wanted to talk to a professional about them. I haven't changed my mind, if that's what you're thinking."

"It wasn't."

"Then why did you take the morning off?"

"I wasn't sure I'd be able to move after jogging with you."

The smile that spread over his face took the innuendo out of his words, but Meghan wondered if there was a double meaning lurking in there anyway.

"What were your questions?" he asked.

"They weren't that serious. I just wanted to understand what was involved, how long the procedure takes, those kinds of things."

Meghan thought back to yesterday. The Newburg Fertility Center was housed in a beautiful old redbrick building in downtown Baltimore. A grand circular archway welcomed visitors and employees to what once had been a single-family home. The inside had been cut up, renovated, redone, made over, until all but one vestige of the original interior remained. Only the outside facade remained intact. And thankfully, no one had ever decided to carve a name into the frieze. Only a staked sign in the ground outside indicated the address.

The directory inside listed the vast number of businesses and their subsequent suite numbers.

Meghan knew which suite she was going to. Number 305. She took the staircase. It was the one item inside that remained unchanged. It wound up both sides of the grand foyer to a landing and then continued upward to the second floor. To reach Suite 305, she had to go up another level that was at the end of a long hall. Offices flanked one side and an overlook of the floor below the other.

Meghan had carefully researched this fertility center. The Internet was full of information. And she found a forum where she could ask questions. She'd joined under an alias and had been on it almost exclusively for days. She'd met a group of women she never knew existed. They'd given her advice and cautions. They'd even invited her to join them for a face-to-face meeting. Meghan thought better of that. She didn't need them finding out that she was the fiancée of Thomas Worthington-Yates.

She turned the handle of a dark wood door with Suite 305 in gold lettering on it. The inside was bright and cheery, with light blue wallpaper and chairs covered in a coordinating fabric. There were no other patients waiting.

"Ms. Howard?" the receptionist greeted her with a smile.

Meghan nodded. She immediately understood that there were never any waiting patients. Appointments were staggered so there would be no overlap.

"You can come right in," the receptionist said.

Like magic the door at the end of the wall opened and a uniformed nurse waited for her. Meghan was ushered into an office where a kind older man stood up and clasped her hand.

"Please be seated," he said.

Dr. Rayford Armstrong was in his fifties. He had silver hair, blue eyes that were tinged with gray and soft hands. He stood only an inch or so above her five feet six inches.

Meghan took a seat and looked at him across his clean desk.

"I'll run through the procedure, tell you the success and failure rates, what you can expect. If you have any questions, interrupt at any time." He spread his hands in an inviting gesture, then steepled them as if he needed time to get his thoughts together.

He started, explaining how the frozen embryo would be implanted. They usually used several embryos, to raise the probability of success, but obviously this was a special exception.

"Meghan?" Thomas called her name.

She'd forgotten he was there. Dr. Armstrong had been kind and convincing. He worked with many surrogates and wanted her to be comfortable with her decision.

"I asked about the confidentiality of my identity and yours, although I never mentioned your name," Meghan said.

"Is that where you want to go?"

"When I have it done?"

He nodded.

"I haven't decided. I thought I'd discuss it with you. You and Ruth used another clinic. Do you want to maintain the relationship there?"

"It wasn't a relationship and I think wherever you go should be someplace that *you* have confidence in."

"The doctor said there is a preparation period. There are tests, hormones and injections I have to take over a period of time before the implantation."

He nodded. *He knew it all too well,* Meghan thought.

"Have you thought about how you'll feel if this doesn't work?" Meghan asked.

"Is that what this is all about? Fear? Are you afraid?"

"A little," she said. "Aren't you?"

He glanced down, then back at her. "I'm terrified," he admitted. "Until Nina and Adam started this downhill train, I'd pushed the thought to the back of my mind. Now it's the only thing I think about."

"So what will you do if it doesn't work? The doctor told me the chances of one embryo being successful are very low."

Thomas waited a long moment. Meghan watched him, watched the play of emotions on his face. After a while, she didn't think he was going to answer. He had no answer. He clearly wanted this child as much as he wanted to breathe.

"I honestly haven't thought of that. I refuse to let myself go there. But I guess I'll have to live with it."

Meghan hadn't thought of this being emotional when she and Thomas had first met. They were clearly on opposite sides. She never expected to see him except when absolutely necessary. Even though she insisted they marry, and they would occupy the same house, he was a workaholic. The marriage was in name only, so she would live in a nice house for nine months with only a little contact. Then she would begin the next phase of her life.

But already Thomas was part of her life. With that came responsibilities, emotional responsibilities. And she found herself getting more emotionally involved than she had bargained for. She knew she would have to deal with the feelings, but what kept coming back to her were the doctor's last words.

She'd reached over to shake his hand and thank him. "You haven't asked me the questions most women want to know," he said.

Meghan stared at him, unable to think of any other questions.

"The one on sex," he supplied.

She was unsure which emotion racked her body— fear, hope, need—but she'd felt hot blood inch up her neck and knew her skin tone had darkened.

"What about sex?" she ventured.

"It's permissible. Before the implantation. It won't reduce the chance of pregnancy. In fact, the opposite is the case."

Meghan could hardly control her breath. Images of herself and Thomas naked on a bed flashed so suddenly into her head that she'd reached for her bottle of water to cool the internal furnace that counteracted the air-conditioned room.

As she looked at Thomas now, that same furnace kicked on and rapturous images flooded her mind, and nothing could block out the image of his powerful body or her thoughts of being enfolded intimately within it.

* * *

"Suzanne, it's good to see you." Meghan rushed forward and hugged her sister as she came through the security checkpoint at BWI Airport. "You've lost weight." Meghan tightened her grasp. She was surprised at how much she had missed her sister.

"I live in California. You know that do-as-the-natives-do thing and all…" Suzanne laughed as she spoke. "I missed you, too. I'm so excited about being back. This side of the world is so different from California."

"Yeah," Meghan said. "The water is on the east." It was a joke they used to use when Suzanne said she was accepting a job in Los Angeles.

"For one thing." Suzanne gave the response to the saying.

Suzanne looked a lot like Meghan, despite them having different fathers. They both had long dark hair, although Meghan's fell past her shoulders and Suzanne's was threatening the middle of her back. They had similar bone structure and eyebrows that arched like their mother's.

"I can't get over it," Meghan said. "It's only been a few months and you look like the west coast really agrees with you." They joined the crowd headed toward baggage claim. Meghan surveyed her sister. Her skin glowed. Golden brown and healthy. She walked with an air of confidence that Meghan hadn't noticed before. Men's heads turned and appreciative smiles curved their lips as they passed. Suzanne didn't appear to notice.

"You look more relaxed," Suzanne said. "Do we have Mr. Wonderful to thank for that?"

"Mr. Wonderful," Meghan said, laughing. "He's anything but that." Meghan didn't know why she said that. She had never kept a secret from Suzanne, but she didn't want anyone to know how much she liked Thomas. He was much the same person he'd been as a teenager, but he was so much more now that both mind and body were in sync with each other.

They made their way down the escalator and into the large room with conveyor belts that snaked in and out and around the place. Electronic boards showed the flight numbers. They stood waiting and watching as bags began to circle the slow merry-go-round.

"Let me see it," Suzanne said.

"See what?"

"What do you think? The ring."

Meghan raised her hand. She still twisted the gold band constantly. Suzanne probably noticed Meghan fiddling with it.

"Good grief," she said. "I could skate on that."

Meghan blushed. "I tried to talk Thomas into something smaller, but…" She looked down at the stone.

"You love it." Suzanne finished her sentence.

Meghan looked up at her sister. For a moment she said nothing. Feeling the smile curling her mouth up, she said, "I love it."

"He sure sounds like Mr. Wonderful to me. I can't wait to meet him."

Suzanne always over-packed. Meghan watched two suitcases come off the conveyor belt. Along with the carry-on she was pulling, that made three bags. They'd been a graduation gift from her when Suzanne accepted the job in California.

"How long are you staying?" Meghan asked when Suzanne identified the third bag.

"Until the wedding."

"That's three weeks away, if all goes well. What about your job?"

"They'll survive without me. And I took all the vacation I had coming to me."

Meghan understood the significance of the survive statement. She'd taken her job seriously. She was always there, rarely taking sick days or even mental health days.

"You didn't expect me to leave when your life is about to go through a major upheaval, did you?"

Meghan's footsteps echoed on the parking-lot pavement as they pulled the suitcases to the waiting car.

"How did you get to be so wise?" Meghan asked, putting the suitcases in the trunk of the car.

"I have a very wise big sister." Suzanne smiled. "She taught me everything I know."

Meghan stopped what she was doing and looked at her sister. She was very proud of Suzanne. After they lost their parents, their lives could have taken a wrong turn, but they'd survived and both were independent now.

"Thank you," Meghan said, uttering the words softly, but the impact of them was monumental.

Her sister was all grown up. For so long Meghan had thought of her as her little sister, but she would never think of her that way again. Her fledgling had wings. She could fly solo.

"What did you mean back there when you said 'if all goes well'?"

"Nothing, really," Meghan said. She was sorry she'd said it out loud.

"Meghan," Suzanne said, a warning note in her voice. "I'm a grown-up now. You don't have to protect me."

"I'm not protecting you." Meghan glanced at her before turning her attention back to the Parkway traffic.

"Then answer my question."

"There's a lot involved in this process and it might not work. In fact, the probability of it *not* working is higher than it working."

"So, what happens if it doesn't?" Suzanne's face had morphed into a mask of concern.

"I'll be all right." Meghan hadn't shared the exact terms of her and Thomas's agreement with her sister. "I'll have time to find another job and get back on my feet."

"Is that part of the arrangement you've agreed to?"

Meghan nodded. She wasn't going to elaborate. Suzanne seemed to understand that, because she changed the subject.

"So, tell me about him." Suzanne glanced out the window. The broadleaf trees along the Baltimore-Washington Parkway sped by as Meghan drove toward the city and home. At least for the next three weeks it was home.

"I don't know a lot about him. Most of what I know came from reading newspapers and magazines," Meghan stated. She left out the talks they'd had in either her home or his.

"You're too sensible to agree to this change of life-style without knowing anything about the man. So, let's start with what he looks like. Is he a staid businessman, or a royal hunk?"

Meghan didn't often think of the age difference between herself and Suzanne. But she could see it now in the gestures of her talkative sister.

"Are those my only two choices?"

"Is there anything in between?"

"Maybe not in California, but this is Baltimore and we have a wide variety of personality types here."

"I've seen his picture," Suzanne told her. "I looked him up on the Internet. But you know those pictures, even with the best resolution, can't tell you what a living, breathing person is like. Although I'd place him in the royal hunk category on looks alone."

"He's very nice-looking," Meghan conceded.

"I could see that."

"He's very into his business. And he wants a child."

"You don't want children," Suzanne said. "You always said that. Of course, I didn't believe you. You were too good a mother to me. Have you changed your mind?"

Meghan shook her head. "It's still true." She tried to say it lightly. "I'm doing this because I lost my job and they aren't easy to come by at this time and after the surrogacy I can return to school and eventually get a better job."

"You said that on the phone."

Suzanne was scrutinizing her. Meghan couldn't do much but withstand it. She was driving and needed to keep her attention on the road.

"Are you sure you want to do this, Meghan?" Suzanne paused. "I know we didn't have it easy growing up. You had it worse than I did. You had to contend with me."

"You were never a burden," Meghan said.

"But I held you back."

"No, you—"

"Don't say that because I did and I know it. If Mom and Dad had lived, you could have done anything you wanted. You might even have been married by now. And you wouldn't have to do this just to go back to school."

"I'm not doing this just to go back to school." Meghan glanced at her sister. "I can enroll in night school. It would take longer to graduate, and I'd have to find a job to supplement my income. This is a job. That's how I'm looking at it. And I don't regret one minute of our lives. I wish Mom and Dad had lived, but we can't change what happened. And I'm not that old. After this year, I can resume my life. I can do whatever I want, just like you said. Plus, I'd really be helping someone in need."

"Are you sure? Living with a man is different than living with your sister."

"And how would you know that?"

"Don't change the subject," Suzanne said. "And for the record, no, I am not living with anyone."

"Have you met someone?"

"Didn't you hear me?" Suzanne said a little louder. "We're not changing the subject."

Meghan nodded.

"Something could happen to the two of you in a year."

"Suzanne, this is not a movie. There will be no swell of music at the end of the year. No credits will roll as we discover our love for each other and kiss as the screen fades to black."

"Don't be too quick to dismiss that. Why do you think movies end like that? Because there's truth in them."

"A grain of truth," Meghan reminded her. "Most of them are fantasy, at least the ones with the swell of music and the star-crossed lovers at the end."

"You could be star-crossed, too," Suzanne whispered. Meghan felt her comment was almost a suggestion.

"Are you saying you don't think I could fall in love?"

"No, I'm saying you won't let yourself. Don't make him one of your cases. You've been taking care of me, taking care of the foster kids and abused kids and other people in need. You don't let yourself have time for you."

Meghan was poised to deny it, but then saw the truth in her sister's words.

"Give yourself a chance, Meghan. After this year is over, forget everyone else, even me, and live for Meghan."

Meghan pulled the car to a stop in front of their house. "I'll give it some thought," Meghan said. Then she smiled. "And you'll be on the top of my list of people to forget."

The offices of Worthington-Yates Investments took up the fourteenth floor of the Roxbury Building near the Baltimore Harbor. From Thomas's office window he had a panoramic view of traffic on the waterway. Sitting in his big leather chair, his hands steepled in thought, he watched the water flow. Somewhere out there, he thought, was Meghan Howard, the future mother of his child. He shook his head. Meghan was not the mother. Ruth was the real mother. Meghan was the incubator, a loaner body to carry and birth a child he'd conceived with the woman he loved.

Thomas told himself this. He'd been silently repeating it ever since that night on her porch—and yesterday and the day before. Ever since he'd taken her in his arms and kissed her, held her thin body against his and felt every line and curve of her build.

Meghan wasn't his type, yet he found himself thinking of her more and more. He shifted and looked at Ruth's photo on his desk. She smiled at him, offering him nothing in the way of advice. She neither approved nor disapproved of his decisions, yet he felt his allegiance to her ebbing. That bothered him.

He'd given himself boundaries and for years he'd adhered to them. But his life was changing while hers remained constant in the photo frame. His chain links were melting in the heat of need and the feeling of protection that he felt for Meghan.

He was forming a bond with Meghan, an emotional connection that seemed to grow stronger each time he was in her presence. He wasn't sure if he wanted this connection to go forward, to follow its course to a natural conclusion.

He'd been devastated when Ruth died. Without his in-laws, the three of them dependent on each other, supporting their grief like a three-legged stool, Thomas would have fallen apart and so would they.

Looking away from Ruth, he spied the report lying on his desk. In fact, two reports lay there. His and hers. Meghan had sent a copy of her investigation to him. He hadn't thought to do the same for her.

There was nothing disturbing in hers. She wasn't a model citizen, yet she cared about people. She had no criminal record, not even a traffic ticket or evidence of an overdue library book. He hadn't expected one. She'd been very popular in college, but after her parents died, it was like she died, too.

Thomas could identify with that. Ruth's passing had taken his will to live, too. Had it not been for Adam and Nina, he didn't know what he would have done. Meghan had no one to lean on. She had also taken custody of her young sister. Her neighbors loved her and looked out for her safety.

Thomas admired her. She'd finally reached a point where she could focus on herself and then she'd lost her job. Thomas opened his folder and read through it again. It gave the rudiments of her life, the facts of her existence, but not the essence of it.

Each time he talked to her he learned more about her, about the way she thought and felt. That's really what he wanted to learn from the report, but he knew now that no report could delve into the inner personality of another individual. There was so much about her he didn't know. There was much about him that she didn't know. He'd read his own report and while it gave facts and figures of his life, it only skimmed the surface of who he was. He and Meghan were going to share the same living space for nine months. He was sure that in time they would know each other better.

"Thomas," his secretary said through the intercom. "Ms. Howard is here if you have a few moments."

Thomas's body immediately lurched. His heart thumped at the idea of conjuring her up from his thoughts.

"Send her in." He got up and started for the door when it opened. A woman he didn't recognize came through the door. She was clearly not Meghan. For a moment Thomas was disappointed. He searched for his fiancée and saw her come in behind the stranger. His heart lifted. Unsure of who the woman was with Meghan, Thomas slipped into his role. His arm went around Meghan's waist and he greeted her with a smile and a kiss.

Meghan stepped out of his arms. "This is my sister, Suzanne," she introduced.

Thomas gazed at Suzanne. Her face glowed from a California sun that had added a layer of coppery color to her skin and highlighted hair, bringing out the reddish tone. His gaze moved from one sister to the other, but after a moment, he stepped forward and shook Suzanne's hand.

"I'm so glad to meet you," he said.

"We're going to be in-laws," Suzanne said. "That deserves a hug." Impulsive as always, Suzanne stepped forward and quickly hugged Thomas.

"I expected you two to look more alike," Thomas said when she moved away.

"Different fathers," Suzanne explained. "But that doesn't keep us from being sisters."

Thomas knew they were close. From the few times Meghan had mentioned her sister, he understood that they loved each other deeply. He'd never had a sibling, although he had a few friends who were as close as brothers.

"Since you're here, why don't we get some lunch?"

"We didn't want to take you away from your work," Meghan stated.

"It can wait," he replied. "I don't often get to spend time with two beautiful women."

He watched Meghan. Under her skin a flush of color washed up her face. She was beautiful. He remembered the teenager she was. Pretty, yes, a little nervous and clumsy, but she'd blossomed into a swan. And she did things to him that no other woman had been able to do since Ruth. She'd quietly broken through his defenses. When she'd first refused his request, it had been a hit to his ego. He wasn't used to refusal. Then he got to know her and found a quiet strength and intelligence that he admired.

As they went through the door, he put his hand on her back. It seemed natural. He didn't even realize he was doing it until he felt her warmth through the fabric of her dress. He liked touching her, wanted to do it more. At odd times he'd find himself thinking of her or dreaming of doing things with her to the point that his body grew hard.

He dropped his hand, recognizing that now was not the time to allow those thoughts to take control. He pushed the button to summon the elevator, but removing his hand from the place it wanted to be took an effort greater than he imagined. He thought of Ruth, tried to pull her image into focus. She was the safe haven for his emotions. But Meghan's presence, the soft scent of her perfume, the way she smiled, the sensual way she moved, conspired to prevent his attention from sharpening on anyone but her.

After a moment, Thomas gave up the effort. Across the small space of the elevator he watched his fiancée. Other than Suzanne, two of his colleagues had stepped into the tiny room when the door slid open. Thomas paid no attention to them. His eyes were only on Meghan.

And for the first time, he didn't care who knew it.

Chapter 8

The room was a maze of boxes. Everywhere Meghan turned she had to weave her way through them. How had she accumulated all this *stuff?* she wondered, carrying a heavy box of books. There was a storage unit, a huge white storage box, in her backyard that she, Suzanne, and several of her neighbors were systematically filling with the memories of her life. Trophies from school days, photographs, clothes, furniture, books, all went into the huge white coffin. It represented the transition her life was taking. She was leaving the old Meghan forever and moving into a new adventure.

She was both excited and afraid. Never in her dreams did she believe she would agree to marry a man she didn't know, let alone love. Or that she would be a surrogate. But as she had learned at an early age, life didn't go according to a preset plan.

She set the box she was carrying on top of two others and turned to reenter the house. The only thing she couldn't put in the portable storage device was the joy she and Suzanne had shared in the tiny rooms that had been their home for over ten years. Suzanne's sweet sixteen party had taken place there. Several of her friends had shown up dressed like the women in *Dreamgirls* and sang a rendition of the musical's songs.

Meghan's twenty-fifth birthday, when she'd been surprised with a ticket to a ski trip by her colleagues and her sister, took place in the dining room. Graduation day, summers sitting on the back porch listening to music, simple events that made up daily life, were all part of the rugs, the drywall and the light fixtures. There were so many good times to recall and none of them could be captured and held in the physical confines of the rectangular module.

"Do you want this china in there?" Bob Lewis, a blond, college-professor type, asked. He was Suzanne's age and had had a crush on her since puberty. Unfortunately Suzanne's tastes ran toward the hard-bodied, intelligent-model type. Bob held a box labeled "China."

"There's a special shelf for that one," Meghan told him. She led him to the storage unit and showed him the place where the china would be strapped in for transport.

As they walked back into the house, Suzanne approached them. "What time is Thomas coming?" she asked Meghan.

Consulting her watch, Meghan said, "In an hour."

"You should get dressed. We can handle the rest of this." She glanced at Bob, who looked as if she'd agreed to marry him.

"I have a little time."

Meghan got another box and headed back for the storage device. She was moving soon. She wondered what life would be like in a place she'd only dreamed of living. And with Thomas. The reality of this quasi-marriage was proving to be more complicated than she'd pictured. Meghan picked up another box of books and headed for the unit. *Was she falling for Thomas?* She shook her head, refusing to answer that. She couldn't fall for him. It wasn't part of the plan.

Forcing herself to keep sight of that, she put the box down. Twenty minutes later, she headed for the stairs and her bedroom. It was almost time for Thomas to arrive.

"Bob and the rest of us are going to run over to Macchio's and have a pizza. We can finish the rest tomorrow."

"Have a good time," Meghan said.

Suzanne smiled and went out the door. Meghan was hot and sweaty from the exertion of packing. The house was now comfortably quiet with the cessation of movement. Stepping on the first rung of the stairs, she thought of Thomas. He was taking her to get the marriage license. It was becoming real, Meghan thought. Running up the steps, she walked into her bedroom. She needed to shower and change. Each time she showered, she was reminded that Thomas had been in there, too. He'd used her bathroom two days in a row. She was sure that although she couldn't see him, she could feel that he'd been there. His scent wafted through the small room.

Meghan went into the shower with a light step and a wide smile, knowing she was safe wrapped in his ethereal arms.

"What's this?" Thomas asked, when Meghan called for him to come in. Coming in from the kitchen, she saw him walking around the boxes.

"We were packing, but the heat got the better of the crew and they went for pizza and cold drinks."

"Packing?"

She laughed. He probably thought she was planning to move all this stuff to his manicured neighborhood.

"We're putting it in storage until I get a new apartment," she explained.

"I should have thought of that," he said. "Can I help with something?"

"We'll finish it tomorrow. We'd better get to the license bureau before it closes."

He nodded, taking a step. He expected Meghan to fall into step with him, but she didn't move. Thomas stared at her. The mood in the room changed. They'd been speaking easily, but now a cloying cloud of doubt washed over her.

"What's wrong?" he asked.

"Do you really want to do this?" she asked.

"It was your idea," he replied.

"I understand that, but we're nearing a point of no return. We haven't gotten there yet, but if you're having second thoughts, I need to know."

"I'm not."

"You want this baby bad enough to marry me to get it?"

It sounded like a trick question. Either answer would be wrong. Yet Thomas's head bobbed slowly up and down. She saw him swallow. She'd been trained to read body language, but she didn't know what that meant.

"What about you? Do you want your new life, your school and career this badly?"

Meghan did. She was tired of struggling, tired of penny pinching and tired of going without. She only had to wait several months for her new life to begin.

"I haven't changed my mind," she answered.

Thomas took the two steps that brought him close to her. He stopped close enough for their toes to touch. "Maybe we'd better go, then."

But they didn't move toward the door. Thomas leaned forward, his finger lifting her chin until his mouth hovered over hers. He didn't kiss her, although there was only a millimeter of air separating his lips from hers. Meghan felt the fire. Her bones melted. To keep her balance, she reached for him, her arms running around his tight waist. His went around her, embracing her in a clasp as strong as steel.

No words were spoken, none were needed. His mouth brushed hers. Back and forth their lips painted each other's. Meghan's arms moved with a mind of their own, exchanging positions until they wound around his neck. She pulled his head down to meet her mouth. Fire erupted around them. Thomas pulled her as close to him as he could get her. Meghan felt the hard length of him, knew the arousal of his body as it fit into hers.

They exchanged positions, their heads moving back and forth as they responded to the inciting need growing in each other.

"This is crazy," he whispered against her mouth.

"I know," Meghan said, her mouth feathering his with whispery kisses. She ignored the voice in her head that brought back the memory that she and Thomas would not do this again. She couldn't stop herself. Each time she saw him, she wanted to run her hands all over his body. She wanted to slowly remove his clothes, revealing his perfect body one brown inch at a time.

"If you want me to stop…" Thomas's voice was deep and breathless. "Now would be the time to say something."

Meghan answered with her mouth. And her hands. And her body. She went up on her toes, pressing herself even closer to him. The kiss deepened, taking on a new level. His tongue dug deep into her mouth. Meghan had never felt so alive, so close to another human being. Her body was humming, vibrating, breaking apart except for a thin layer of burning skin that kept her from shattering.

Meghan had taken care with her wardrobe, choosing a white suit with a violet shell and matching shoes. Thomas removed the jacket, slipping it down her arms while his fingers burned a trail from her shoulders to her hands. Then he slipped his hands under the stretchy fabric spanning her waist.

Meghan moaned as naked skin touched naked skin. Her stockinged leg wrapped around his. His erection pressed into her. She felt a wetness in her panties. Thomas unbuttoned her blouse and lowered the zipper on her skirt.

Meghan's hands loosened his tie, pulled it down and off. The buttons on his shirt opened with little effort and she pressed her splayed fingers against his damp skin.

Inhaling, she took in the essence of him, kissing his chest, feathering it with her mouth from one side to the other. Running her tongue over his flat nipples, she tasted the saltiness of his skin, felt his surprised reaction and moaned when his hands pressed her buttocks and her body against his erection.

Thomas reached down, his hands stealing behind her knees as he lifted her. He carried her up the stairs, keeping her balanced even though his mouth stayed glued to hers all the way to her bedroom. The bed gave as he lay her on it. His eyes, warm and brilliant with desire, devoured her face, imprinting it on his mind.

Slowly his hands began an exploration of her body as his passion deepened to meet hers and he quickly undressed her.

"Thomas…I…" Meghan whispered.

"Don't talk." Thomas stopped her, his voice husky. "Don't talk, don't think, just feel." His soft voice was her undoing. She reached up to pull his mouth back to hers hearing a low moan in his throat before restraint snapped in him. His hands caressed her body from head to foot, light fingers ran over her curves causing tiny fires to ignite along the trails his fingers traversed. She in turn memorized every inch of his taut body pressing her lips to his shoulder. She trembled as his body covered hers.

Feeling the total length of him covering her slender frame. She was afraid, wanting to push him away, but the sensations his hands were causing as they trailed fires along her arms, her throat, her breasts, quickly left her a mindless mass of emotion. Slowly he intensified her desire, finding every erotic area while his tongue and hands exploited them to the point of an exquisite, physical pain—a pain so sweet she shuddered, arching herself closer to him.

Thomas made love to her slowly, entering her slight body for the first time with such tenderness she could hardly express herself without tears. Settling into a rhythm, they began their seductive dance. Meghan murmured his name over and over, unable to refrain from doing it. He was totally in her, engulfed in a world of sensation and need, consumed by a feeling of intense pleasure such as she had never known.

Totally mindless now, she writhed beneath the heightened rhythmic thrust of his taut body. They soared, her hands moving on his powerful body as she moaned incoherently into his shoulder.

His mouth covered hers again as they came to a final shuddering climax. Clinging to each other, savoring the sweet moment as long as possible, Meghan kissed his shoulder, while his arms tightened around her, gathering her closer to him. Tears streamed from her eyes. It was beautiful, the most beautiful experience she had ever known or imagined. She was overcome with the force of emotion that welled up inside her.

Thomas was kissing her again, their bodies connected, consumed with feelings that only two people could understand, glad he was a man and she was a woman.

Finally they both lay exhausted in each other's arms. He looked at her—his Meghan, her eyes shining and drowsy. He gathered her even closer to him and studied her face. Meghan knew her skin was flushed with color, that her body was slightly moist with perspiration, her beautiful hair almost obscuring the pillow she rested on. She didn't know how beautiful she looked to Thomas. She knew he wanted her and she wanted him. She wanted to wake next to him each day, spend her life drowning in his smile and she wanted to be rewarded by this look after making love, to see it shining in his eyes, to bear his children, to be his wife. Reverently he kissed her forehead and contentedly fell asleep.

A restful and dreamless sleep claimed Meghan, a sleep of contentment she had not experienced before. When she woke it was dark. Thomas was dressed, sitting on the side of the bed watching her. She sighed, stretching lazily.

"How long have you been watching me?" She smiled at him.

"Not long," he answered quietly.

"Are you leaving?"

"In a few minutes," he replied. They had long since missed the license bureau. He pulled Meghan into his arms and cradled her there as if she were a newborn baby. Meghan thought of bearing his child, watching as the head crowned and she saw the first vestige of hair.

Then she remembered the real reason she was with Thomas. And like their climax, her world shattered.

The next day, Meghan looked around the empty room. Part of her life lived in the walls and floor of this space. No amount of cleaning and painting would remove the lives that had been spent here.

Leaving was both necessary and bittersweet. Meghan rubbed misty eyes. She knew it was for the best that she not return here after her divorce. She didn't want to have to explain why and how her marriage had failed. When she saw people she knew in the future, she could discuss the school she was attending, her new job or her new apartment. Life changed every day. She was entering a new phase of hers, with only a little regret to what she was leaving behind.

Meghan pulled the door closed and locked it for the last time. Sniffing, she raised her head, adjusted the purse strap on her shoulder and walked down the steps.

The driver came forward and took the things she was carrying, placing them in the car. Evelyn crossed the street and rushed to hug her.

"I'm going to miss you," Evelyn said.

"I'm not going to the moon," Meghan told her. "I'll come back to see you. After all, I'm going to need my hair and makeup done."

"The shore is a long way off. And with that fiancé of yours, you'll be so busy with him that you won't have time to come visit us."

"Evelyn, don't cry." Meghan knew if Evelyn couldn't hold it together, neither could she.

The two of them were joined by Mr. Forrest. He lived next door. Before his wife died, she used to take care of Suzanne while Meghan was at work and Suzanne was still in school. Meghan knew his house as well as she knew her own.

He hugged her, not saying a word.

"Are you going to be all right?" Meghan suddenly felt guilty that she wouldn't be there to check in on him once in a while. He had a son and daughter who came by regularly, but he always smiled when he saw her.

He nodded instead of speaking. She understood his emotion. He rarely showed it, but she knew he thought of her and Suzanne as his daughters.

When she turned around, her other neighbors had joined them. The small circle grew larger. Meghan hugged them, no longer able to stem the tears. Some pulled her hand up to view the huge diamond on her third finger. Others told her to keep in touch, or said they would see her at the wedding.

Suzanne came forward and tapped her on the arm.

"We have to go now." She spoke to the group. Meghan was grateful to her. She'd taken control. Meghan had gotten caught up in the past, her love for her personal world and the fact that she was leaving it behind going almost as far as the moon compared to the where she stood now.

Shepherding her into the car, Suzanne climbed in behind her and the driver closed the door. As they drove away, Meghan refused to look back. She didn't want to see the old neighborhood receding. She could leave it and she knew she wouldn't be returning. When her nine months were over, she would take a place somewhere distant from here. She might even leave the state to attend school.

Her heart was already telling her to get as far away from Thomas as she could.

Chapter 9

Meghan heard the doorbell. Normally, she would get up to answer it, but she'd found out that living in Thomas's house had rules and boundaries that she was not to change. Her position here was temporary.

So Mrs. Barrie, the housekeeper, silently passed the door to the great room where Meghan sat reading, on her way to the front entry hall.

Meghan listened for who was arriving, unannounced, at this time. It was just past lunch. Thomas was working and not expected until well past the normal dinnertime. Suzanne was staying with a friend back in the city. The two had moved in a week ago. The wedding was scheduled for the next week. Meghan wondered if her entire time at Thomas's would be as inactive as the last week had been. Thomas was rarely there. He came on the

weekend and stayed until Sunday night before returning to his apartment in the city.

Meghan felt homeless. She'd given up her rented
house and now the Eastern Shore, with a full view of the
ocean, was her temporary home. She hid her feelings
from Suzanne when she was there. Suzanne was a but-
terfly, flitting from one place to another. She didn't see
how anyone wouldn't be happy in these surroundings,
but Meghan felt like she'd entered a satin-and-velvet-
lined prison.

She could still walk away, although it would be difficult. She'd given up everything. She'd have to start
over and without the hefty increase to her bank account
these next nine months would give her.

When she heard Nina's voice, her heart lifted and she
nearly flew up from her chair. She met Nina in the hall
as she walked slightly behind Mrs. Barrie.

"This is a wonderful surprise," Meghan said as the
two hugged and blew air kisses. "I am so glad to see
you." Then she looked around her. Usually when
Meghan saw Nina, she saw Adam. "Are you alone?"

"I left Adam at home. He hates shopping."

"Shopping?"

"Yes, we have to find you a dress."

"A dress?"

"You haven't forgotten that you're getting married
in a week?"

How could she? Meghan thought. Every day, as she
rambled around the huge house, all she could think
about was her upcoming nuptials. Getting married had
been her idea, her condition. And she had thought of

nothing else since she walked across the threshold, carrying only a small suitcase. The portable storage device had been filled to the edge with the summary of her life. All she brought to Thomas's house was two suitcases and a backpack containing her cosmetics and hair dryer.

"Don't just stand there," Nina said, interrupting her thoughts. "Get your purse. Let's go." She accompanied her command by waving her hands in a pushing motion.

"Nina, I don't want to make a big deal out of this."

"Too late." She brushed aside Meghan's concerns. "You have to consider Thomas. The wedding is scheduled. You need something to wear and clothes to take on your honeymoon."

"Honeymoon?" Thousands of images crowded in her brain, playing out entire sequences of scenes that she had not planned on. She and Thomas had decided on an in-name-only marriage. They didn't need a honeymoon, she thought.

"It's expected," Nina said.

"This is just a marriage of convenience, Nina."

"True, but in order to keep the pretense up, Thomas will have to take you away. And look at you…" Nina swept her eyes up and down Meghan. "Who's going to believe that Thomas wouldn't want to spend a week in bed with you?"

Meghan's face went red-hot. She had no comeback.

"Go. Go," Nina said, clapping her hands and hurrying her along. "We don't have all day."

Meghan did as she was told, taking only a moment to trade her shorts for a pair of slacks and sandals to cover her bare feet. She passed the lip gloss over her mouth, pulled a brush through her hair, and grabbed her purse on the way to the staircase.

Nina was talking to Mrs. Barrie when Meghan came down the stairs. Immediately, she joined Meghan and the two were through the door and into the car as if they needed to escape the house. Meghan admitted sometimes she wanted to escape.

It didn't take long to reach the row of wedding stores. The shore didn't have that many places to buy clothes and all the wedding necessities were concentrated along one row of a side street. There was a bridal shop, tuxedo shop, bakery, three florists, two photographers, a caterer and a real estate office for both summer rentals and reception halls.

Apparently, all the details had been taken care of by Nina, except the dress. Entering the shop, Meghan was transformed. Like Alice in Wonderland, Meghan was a fish out of water. But Nina was a pro. In no time she had Meghan in and out of several gowns. Finally, Meghan let her inhibitions go and joined in the jocularity of shopping for a beautiful gown.

"How does that one fit?" Nina asked through the door of the dressing room.

"It's a little tight."

Meghan opened the door for her future…what? Nina and Adam would not be her in-laws, even though she was beginning to think of them as such.

"Oh, no." Nina frowned. "Take it off. We'll keep looking."

She closed the door to return for more dresses. With only a week to the ceremony, Meghan had no time to order a gown. She had intended to wear a pale blue evening dress that she'd bought years ago, but Nina insisted that she needed a proper dress. And Meghan wouldn't be surprised if Suzanne didn't have a hand in this shopping expedition, too.

Wearing a wrap provided by the shop, Meghan went out to the displays and looked through the gowns. She chose one and pulled it down from the rack. Seeing the sleeves would stop at her elbows, she returned it. She didn't like that style. As she looked up, she got a glimpse of a gown hanging in the back room, behind a partially opened door.

Her breath had only ever been taken away when she saw Thomas for the first time, but the dress had the same effect. She knew it right away. That was the one.

"Is that for sale?" she asked the clerk who was helping them.

The woman nodded. "It's just come in. I haven't had a chance to tag it yet." She glanced at Meghan. Nina joined them. "Would you like to try it on?"

"Yes," Meghan said.

"It was made for you," Nina said when Meghan turned toward the mirror after Nina closed the row of buttons on her back. Meghan stared at herself in the mirror. She couldn't speak. The reflection in the mirror had to be someone else. It couldn't be her. It was a bride, a beautiful bride.

"Try this with it." The clerk handed Nina a veil. Meghan had to stoop down for Nina to place it on her head. When Meghan looked in the mirror again, she was sure she was going to cry.

"Ahhh," Nina breathed. "*This* is the dress."

The two women looked at each other in the mirror. Meghan nodded. The lump in her throat was too large to swallow. She felt like a bride. For a moment she remembered Thomas making love to her. *Was this how a real bride felt? What would Thomas think when he saw her? Would he want her to be his real bride?*

Morning Has Broken. Cat Stevens was singing his signature song on the radio when Meghan opened her eyes. She let it play, listening to the lyrics and feeling as if he was singing directly to her. She'd set the clock to wake up early, although she didn't know why. The ceremony wasn't until five o'clock, but she had an appointment for her hair and nails, compliments of her sister. She also had to pack for a honeymoon. She had no idea where they were going, only that Thomas needed to be back in a week and her implantation procedure was scheduled for two weeks from the wedding. Nine months and two weeks from today she would give birth.

She hadn't gotten much sleep, restless about the wedding and all the faces of strangers she'd have to deceive kept her tossing and turning. When she wasn't thinking about the wedding deception, her mind kept replaying her and Thomas making love. Since she'd come to live in his house, he had touched her only when they had an audience.

Still her body tingled at the thought of that one day. She stretched leisurely, extending her long legs in the queen-size bed until the tucked-in sheets restrained her.

She wondered what Thomas was doing. Did he spend the night as she had, thinking, wondering about her, about their lovemaking? Did he feel the same…she stopped, refusing to give importance to the word. Was he wondering about the wedding today?

"You're awake. Good." Suzanne bounded into the room. She was wearing a nightgown and robe set that she hadn't had when she left the east coast. "We should make this a memorable day."

Meghan sat up. The T-shirt she'd slept in was old and comfortable. Nina had insisted she buy lingerie for the trip. Meghan didn't see a need. The way Thomas was acting, he wouldn't even notice the lingerie *if* he ever saw it.

"It will be memorable, no matter what," Meghan told her.

"I mean do something special, so you can tell my grandchildren about it, since you don't plan to have any after this is over."

"I think this will be as bizarre a story as they need." Meghan tried to laugh. "I have appointments for hair and nails, the same as you. I have to pack and so do you. What could we do that's memorable?"

"I don't know. Maybe we could go to the beach and take pictures, ride into town and have muffin tops for breakfast."

Town was a small collection of shops that sold mainly seasonal gear to the summer residents and tourists.

"Remember when I was small and we used to ride the ferry over to New Jersey and back? We'd buy popcorn on the boat and watch the seagulls flying. They were some of the happiest times."

Meghan stared at her sister. Suzanne walked to the windows and looked out. You could hear the surf in the distance, but not see the water. Meghan didn't know that about Suzanne. She thought the day was just a way to get out of the city and breathe the fresh air. The sun, sand and water helped both of them deal with the grief of losing their mother.

"Okay," Meghan said. "I'll grab a suit and we'll head for the beach."

Suzanne came alive again.

Meghan held up her hand, stopping her sister from forgetting the true plan for the day. "We'll have to be back by noon to keep our appointments."

"I'll get my stuff." Like a bright ball, Suzanne bounced out of the room.

Happy times, Meghan thought. She had been happy on the beach, too. The ferry ride was a wonderful amusement park for them. Meghan suddenly wondered if the child she was to carry and birth would find pleasure in simple sunny days, or would she or he be forever wanting the latest and greatest toy?

She caught herself thinking like an expectant mother, but then remembered her time with the child would end at birth. There was no future, no beach days, no lessons on enjoying the wind and water from her.

This was Thomas's child. His and Ruth's. Meghan was only the incubator. Somehow that made her sad.

Nina and Adam's house was the site of the ceremony. Meghan was relived she would not be in a church. The sun rose high in the sky and no rain clouds threatened.

Flowers abounded in the backyard, transforming the space into a flower garden. Three hundred white chairs had been set up facing a raised platform on which she and Thomas would vow their undying love.

Meghan stood in her dress, a confection of white lace and satin with a boat neck that left her shoulders naked. The sleeves ended in points at her fingers. The veil hung on a stand. She was alone with her thoughts when a soft knock came on the door.

Thinking it was Nina or Suzanne, she said, "Come in."

Thomas opened the door and walked inside. Meghan gasped at how good he looked, wearing a black tuxedo and pink silk tie that matched the dress that Suzanne would wear as Meghan's maid of honor.

It was supposed to be bad luck for the groom to see the bride before the wedding, but they had already arranged to end the marriage before the ceremony. Meghan thought his presence couldn't make a difference to the eventual outcome.

"I don't think you're supposed to be here," she said, lightly admonishing him.

"I know, but I wanted to talk to you."

"Is something wrong?"

He shook his head. "Remember when you said we were nearing the point of no return?"

She nodded. They'd passed that point when they made love. At least she had.

"Today we reach that point. Until the ceremony is over, you can still call it off."

"What will all those people in the white chairs think?"

"Don't worry about them. I want to know that you have no reservations about this."

"None," she said, looking him directly in the eye.

He looked back. A long moment passed before he spoke. "Then I'll see you in fifteen minutes."

She nodded. Thomas turned and walked toward the door. Meghan watched him. She wanted to say something, keep him with her for a few more moments before they had to stand up in front of a crowd of nameless faces.

"Oh," he said, turning back. "I almost forgot." He pulled a small oblong box out of his pocket and extend it toward her. "This is for you."

"Why?" she asked, not taking it.

"It's tradition, isn't it? The groom gives the bride a gift on their wedding day."

"I have nothing for you." She felt guilty.

"That's all right. You're giving me a far greater gift than anything I could give you."

Meghan took the box and slowly opened it. When the spring lock flipped open, inside was a beautiful emerald bracelet. Meghan gasped, stepping back as if she could put distance between herself and the hand holding the box.

"This is too much," she said. "I can't accept this."

"Happy wedding day," was all Thomas said before turning and leaving her alone. Alone, with a bracelet that looked like green fire, Meghan was reminded of the fire that only lovemaking could produce.

The ceremony was short, but the day took on a surreal quality. From Meghan dressing in the gown Nina had insisted she accept to the doors opening and Meghan finding a yard full of people. On short notice, she would have thought only fifty or so people would attend the ceremony, but from her tenuous walk down the aisle, she was sure every invitation had been accepted.

Bob Lewis gave her a reassuring smile from the side of the aisle near the back. She smiled and relaxed a little bit. Her hand was wrapped around the arm of Mr. Forrest, her next-door neighbor, who had agreed to give her away. He'd always been a father figure to her and Suzanne. He stared directly in front of him, more nervous than Meghan.

Suzanne stood at the altar as the only bridesmaid and Adam stood up as Thomas's best man. Evelyn and Nina cried from their mother-of-the-bride-and-groom seats. Meghan glanced at them as she went by. She was frightened. Thomas had offered her the final chance to back out of the wedding. As Mr. Forrest relinquished her hand, passing it over to Thomas, she knew she was now committed.

Thomas's hand was as cold as Meghan's as they took their vows. He kissed her softly on the cheek at the end and they turned to greet the crowd. Meghan felt guilty for agreeing to love, honor and cherish when she knew her position as wife was only temporary.

Now, at the reception, she went through the motions. Thomas took her around, introducing her to guests she had not met previously. In turn she introduced him to her friends and former coworkers. Nina and Adam looked the glorious and loving couple.

The reception line, first dance, cutting the cake and throwing the garter and bouquet all passed in a soft blur for Meghan. She was relieved to get away from the well-wishers to change her clothes. The blue suit had called to her when she saw it in the store. She chose it to travel in, exchanging her wedding gown for the short jacket, Bermuda shorts and flat sandals.

She was already packed. Suzanne and Nina had seen to that. Only a few toiletries needed to be added to her bag and she could leave for her honeymoon. Meghan had not expected to go on one. She thought Thomas might stay home a few days to give the appearance that they had gone away, but he had airline tickets and had rented a suite in Acapulco.

"Ready?"

Meghan's head snapped up. Thomas stood in the doorway of the bedroom she'd spent the night and dressed in. While Meghan had told Nina it wasn't necessary since this marriage was doomed to fail from the start, she and Suzanne conspired against her and she'd stayed the night. He'd changed, too, giving up his tux for a polo shirt, sport jacket and khaki pants.

"I am now," Meghan said as she zipped the suitcase closed. He came forward and lifted it off the bed. At the door, he set it in the hall.

"Just one more thing." She picked up the gown she'd worn and carefully returned it to the hanger and the protective bag she'd been given at the bridal shop. It was the most beautiful thing she'd ever owned. And she'd never get to wear it again.

"Ready?" Thomas repeated.

She took his arm and they descended the stairs, returning to the party that was in full swing on the make-

shift dance floor that had been set up on the back lawn.
Couples danced to band music and the flow of champagne. They looked as if they were having a wonderful
time. Suzanne waved to her as she danced with Bob.
Nina and Adam were talking to Mr. Forrest.

The music ended. Adam walked to the bandstand
and took the microphone. "Ladies and gentlemen," he
announced. "The bride and groom, Mr. and Mrs.
Thomas Worthington-Yates." His arm extended in a
flourish. The crowd applauded as Thomas's hand supported Meghan's back and they walked a few steps to
the stand before the crowd. Digital cameras appeared
from pockets, purses or dangling from wrists like old-
fashioned dance cards. Meghan smiled as flashes
snapped and apertures opened and closed.

From somewhere in the back of the crowd the sound
of spoons tapping against crystal glasses grew into high-
pitched musical notes. Traditionally, that sound indicated that the bride and groom should kiss. This was the
fourth time today Meghan had heard it and each time
Thomas had kissed her lightly on the mouth. Roars and
applause bursts from the wedding guests.

This time he turned her into his arms and kissed her
soundly. Meghan's legs grew weak. He'd only kissed her
like this twice before, once at her door and when they made
love. Her hands caught his biceps and she held on until her
released her. As they turned back, Thomas kept her arm
clasped through his and she was grateful for the support.

After a few more minutes of modeling for the
clicking cameras, Suzanne broke free of the crowd and
came forward. Nina and Adam followed her.

"Do you have everything you need?" Suzanne asked.

Meghan nodded. Thomas dropped her arm to shake hands with several people who'd come forward. Meghan felt a rift at the loss of his strength.

"It's time to go, or you'll miss your plane," Nina said in the commanding way she had when she'd took charge.

Meghan looked at her sister. Suzanne was staying one more night and returning to California in the morning. This was the last time she would see her for a while. She hugged her. "Have a safe trip back," she whispered.

They separated. "Call me when you get home."

The comment was automatic. They'd always said it when one of them was going away. Home was where Meghan would be or Suzanne would be. When she and Thomas returned, she wouldn't be going home. She would be returning to his house. She shrugged it off, thinking there were too many people capturing her image for her to allow the strained emotion to be reflected on her face.

"I will," Meghan answered uncertainly.

"Don't worry about me," Suzanne said, tuned into Meghan's thoughts as if she could read her mind. "Nina and Adam are seeing me off and I'll let them know I arrived safely."

Meghan hugged her again. Then Nina and Adam took their turns. The small group waved goodbye. Followed to the waiting car by well wishes, they left for their mock honeymoon.

Meghan sagged against the soft upholstery of the limousine as the driver backed down the long driveway. Unlike a normal bride and groom, she and Thomas didn't sit touching, hugging or kissing, happy to finally be alone on the first day of their marriage. The two sat separated.

"Tired?" Thomas asked.

"A little," she said. "Glad it's over. I feel a little guilty at deceiving all those people."

"I understand."

Meghan glanced at him. She'd been so self-centered that she hadn't thought he might have feelings, too.

"Do you regret marrying me?"

Turning to her as if his head had been pulled by a puppeteer, he stared at her. "Let's not begin this marriage with that as an obstacle," he told her. "We're both doing this for different reasons. I don't regret the decision."

Meghan didn't feel comforted by his words. He wanted a baby and he was willing to do anything to get it. And marrying her had been the first step toward that goal. She needed to keep that in mind. The fact that they'd succumbed to emotions that had them making love didn't enter into it. There was no growing love between them.

Like the contoured seats they occupied, their reasons were separate. And if her feelings for him were spilling into the de-militarized zone, his were clear.

Don't fall in love with me.

It was the worst week of her life. Pretense weighed heavily on Meghan. *How could she have mooned over this guy since she was in high school? How could she melt in his arms each time he held her? And how could he ask her to participate in his insane plot?*

Meghan had never come so close to assaulting another human being in her life as she had the first day they walked into the suite where they were to spend their honeymoon.

"Let me get this straight. You want to suspend our agreement for the duration of this week…" she refused to say honeymoon "…and until I go through the procedure."

"We haven't really been following it anyway," Thomas said.

The truth of this didn't make her feel any better. When they had violated the agreement, it had been mutual and fired by an uncontrollable passion. It hadn't been as cold, calculated and disturbing as stating they were going to go through the motions, mainly the sexual motions, of being man and wife until she was pregnant with another woman's baby. Then they would invoke the original agreement again as if they had shut off a water fountain.

Her emotions didn't run that way. He may never want to marry again, he might still be in love with his first wife and only need the sexual release any woman could supply while he pretended she was Ruth, but Meghan wanted a life of her own now. She'd done her duty as mother and parent. From now on, or at least until the end of this farce, it was all about Meghan.

Conflictingly, she wanted what he offered, wanted more than that. She wanted to be held in his arms, to feel his hands touching her, bringing her body to life, to get lost in his kisses and to have them make love as magically as they had done once before. But anger aided her with the knowledge that this was not the purpose of his request. It was pure and simple self-gratification.

"So you want us to start a relationship and then end it a few weeks from now?"

"Isn't that the overall agreement we already have?"

That's when the anger hit her, white hot and raging. Her hands balled into fists so tightly that she felt the pain of her fingernails digging into her flesh.

With supreme effort she forced herself not to scream, but venom soaked every word she said. "So if I put this in language you understand, I should enter into a heartbreak futures investment." She swung around on him as if she were about to attack. And she wanted to, but kept her feet apart and stapled to the floor. "Are you insane? Or do you think I'm the one who's lost my mind? Why would I agree to something as asinine as that?"

He clearly hadn't expected her outburst. "I'm not one to renegotiate the terms of an agreement once I've committed to it, but if this is your deal breaker, then we can return to the States right now and annul this union."

After a moment he shook his head. "I guess I misread you. I thought your feelings were the same as mine. I stand corrected."

He stood up, acknowledged her with a stiff nod and left. His bedroom door closed with a decided click. Meghan dropped into a chair, hot and angry, her body trembling. She grasped the arms to keep her hands from shaking as her body racked with intense emotion.

What did he think she was? How could he have insulted her so? Meghan took several deep breaths, trying to calm herself. It took ten minutes before the shakes stopped and another five minutes before she could move. Getting up, she changed into running shorts, took her room key and went for a jog along the beach. She ran a mile before stopping. Out of breath, she braced her hands on her knees and gulped the air. The terrain was different, giving under her feet and making the run harder than when she traversed the streets of Baltimore. But she was calmer by the time she returned to the hotel.

The suite had an empty feel when she opened the door. Thomas had gone out. Relief went through her. She had a few more minutes before it would be necessary to confront him again. But by the time she had showered and dressed, he still had not returned. An hour later, she'd begun to worry.

Fear of being abandoned took root inside her. Had he left her, returned to the States without her? she wondered in panic. Meghan admonished herself. Thomas wouldn't do that. She'd read the report her investigator had given her. He was a gentleman in most respects. From what she knew of him personally, he was honorable and fair. He would never leave her alone and stranded, no matter how angry he was.

She needed to find him, however. After their argument, she'd gone for a run. *What did he do? What was his outlet for anger?* She'd never seen him angry before, not really angry.

She found him sitting at the restaurant bar. He had a drink in front of him. Approaching him, she glanced at the bartender, hoping he could give her a clue to Thomas's state. He was busy and didn't see her. The stools on either side of him were occupied, but as Meghan neared Thomas, the man on his right paid his tab and left.

"Are you all right?" she asked, slipping into the seat next to him.

Only his head moved, but he swung it around and stared at her, looking her up and down. "I didn't think you would want to talk to me."

"I went for a run. Cleared my head."

His eyebrows rose.

"I haven't changed my mind," she told him, if he thought she'd come to terms with his proposal and was now willing to accept it.

He took a sip of his drink.

"What's that?" she asked.

He slid the glass in front of her. Meghan didn't know the protocol here. If she'd been talking to one of her charges, she'd have lifted the glass and smelled it, but what did she do with a would-be husband?

"Its tonic water, Meghan," Thomas answered. "I haven't been drowning my sorrows in alcohol. I've been waiting for you to eat dinner."

"Me?"

"I assume you're hungry."

She was starving. Meghan hadn't eaten since they boarded the plane and flew from Baltimore to Mexico. Thomas glanced at the waiter, who nodded.

"Your table is ready," the waiter said.

Thomas slipped off of his seat and extended his arm for Meghan to follow him. She moved toward the dining room. Meghan preceded Thomas. Before their encounter in the suite, Thomas would have taken Meghan's arm or placed his hand on her back to guide her. But since their new setup had been defined, he didn't touch her.

Chapter 10

Polite strangers, that was the only term Meghan could use to describe the people she and Thomas had become. They walked around the same suite, had their meals together, but otherwise they could have been two people who'd never met.

Meghan was glad to have the honeymoon over. Her suitcase lay on the bed of the room she was to occupy in Thomas's house. It was a guest suite, complete with a sitting room and a private bathroom. Thomas's room was down the hall. She placed her belongings in the drawers and closet, thankful that her room shared no walls with his.

As she hung a dress in the closet, she heard a soft knock on the door. Tensing, she twisted around.

"Come in," she called, expecting Thomas. Mrs. Barrie came in carrying a tray.

"I thought you might want something to eat," she said with a smile. "Dinner won't be for another few hours."

"Thank you," Meghan told her. "I am hungry, but I don't need to be waited on."

"Did you enjoy your trip?" she asked.

"Yes," Meghan said with a bright smile. Meghan had decided to keep the truth of her honeymoon between herself and Thomas. "Acapulco is as beautiful as the brochures portray it to be. The water is a blue-green color you have to see to believe."

"Maybe I'll get there one day."

"You'll love it," Meghan told her.

"Well, it's a dream," Mrs. Barrie said, shrugging her shoulders. "Dinner is at six," she said and left Meghan to finish unpacking.

Meghan wondered what Mrs. Barrie thought of her and Thomas occupying separate bedrooms. It seemed very Victorian and Mrs. Barrie would certainly think it odd. Meghan snapped the locks on her suitcase and placed it on the closet shelf. It didn't matter what the housekeeper thought. This was the arrangement, and Meghan wasn't changing it.

Enough changes had already taken place and the monumental one would be completed in the next two weeks. If the procedure was a success, she'd be pregnant.

Meghan looked at the tray. It held a turkey sandwich, a small bowl of fresh fruit and a glass of milk. She liked all these things, but Meghan wondered how Mrs. Barrie knew her taste. And besides, this meal was exactly what a pregnant woman should eat as a snack. *Had Thomas said anything to her?* Meghan decided to eat the meal. She *was* hungry and it was delicious.

Collecting the tray, she left the room and headed for the stairs. She'd hidden as long as she could. It was time to act as if everything was fine. Mrs. Barrie accepted the returned dishes and Meghan's thanks.

Then Meghan went to the music room. It was the room she had initially met Thomas in when she came to see him. He was on the phone.

"Nina and Adam," he whispered, covering the receiver. "She's fine," he said. "Acapulco agreed with her. You should see how her skin glows."

He was looking at her as he spoke. Meghan felt her skin grow hot as blood poured under the thin layer and turned her face a shade redder.

"Lunch tomorrow?" His eyebrows raised in question.

Meghan shook her head. "Doctor's appointment," she said.

"Nina, tomorrow's not good. Meghan has an appointment." He listened for a moment, then addressed her directly. "Nina wants to know if you'd like her to go with you."

The line was open. Thomas's hand did not cover the mouthpiece. Meghan spoke lowly, loud enough for him to hear, but not enough for her voice to carry through the receiver.

"I'd like *you* to go with me," she said.

"Nina, I'll be going with Meghan...all right...I will...Goodbye." He replaced the receiver.

"She said to give you her love."

Meghan smiled. She liked Nina immensely. "Did you mean that?"

"What?" he asked.

"That you'd go with me tomorrow?"

"You have a doctor's appointment?"

She nodded. Did he think she would make something like that up? "It's with Dr. Petry." She had been Ruth's doctor. Thomas knew her.

"I thought you wanted to use someone different."

"I might still. Tomorrow will be my first meeting with Dr. Petry. She's already familiar with you. It might be easier and you trust her."

Thomas smiled. It was the first genuine smile she'd seen on his face in seven days.

"Are you sure you have the time? I know you'd planned to return to work tomorrow. You've been away for over a week." He'd taken a couple of days off before the ceremony and then there'd been the week-long honeymoon.

"What time is the appointment?"

"Ten o'clock," she said. "Thomas, I'm a big girl. I can go to the appointment alone. You go to your office. They probably need you and you'll have a ton of work waiting."

He came to her and put his hands on her upper arms. It was the first time he'd touched her in what seemed like years. The back of Meghan's mouth went dry and she nearly leaned into him. She didn't know how much a person could crave another's touch.

"Nothing is more important than going with you," he said.

Meghan knew he meant nothing was more important

than the baby process, but she let herself think he meant being with her for just a moment.

Barely twenty-four hours later, they sat in front of Dr. Lane Petry's desk. She was a short Filipina with an engaging smile. Her hair was jet-black with only a few gray strands. It had been cut into a style that stopped at her nape and enhanced her long neck.

Thomas explained that Meghan was going to be a surrogate for the last embryo.

Dr. Petry looked at her without censure. "Are you aware of the likelihood of failure in this case?"

"It's been explained to me."

"Are you aware of that Mr. Worthington-Yates and his wife really wanted a baby?"

She glanced at Thomas. Her hands twisted in her lap. She touched the rings on her finger. The one had become two.

"Thomas has explained that to me."

She leaned forward in her chair, looking even smaller behind the massive desk. "Have you ever had a baby before?"

"No," Meghan said.

"Have you ever been pregnant? Most gestational carriers have been."

Meghan noticed Thomas waiting for the answer to that question. It wasn't necessary to actually go to term with a pregnancy. She could have had an ectopic pregnancy or aborted a fetus in her past. She'd done neither of those things.

"No," she answered.

Dr. Petry nodded and went on to explain the physical

changes pregnancy would bring and then the psychological effects of surrogacy. They also had a discussion on the way people view surrogates. Dr. Petry told her that even though Maryland was a surrogate-friendly state, she should be prepared for negative comments from people who discovered she was a surrogate. But the benefits were extraordinary.

Meghan asked a few questions and Dr. Petry answered them quickly and efficiently. Then she told her about preparations for the implantation. Much of what she said was a repeat of Meghan's visit with Dr. Armstrong.

"Have you ever been a surrogate before?"

Meghan shook her head.

"How did you come to make this decision?"

Meghan was unprepared for that question. She glanced at Thomas.

"I see you're wearing wedding rings. Have you and your husband discussed the effects this will have on your family?"

"Dr. Petry," Thomas interrupted. "This is a strange situation and I won't go into detail, but Meghan and I were married a week ago."

Meghan searched the doctor's face for some type of sign, but she found none. "I see," she said after a moment. The slowness with which the words came said she didn't see at all. "I guess congratulations are in order."

"Thank you," Thomas said.

She turned to Meghan. "You are aware that you will be having another woman's child?"

"Yes," Meghan said. "I know how much this means to Thomas."

"So you're not a surrogate. You're married and you live together. If this works, you're going to be the child's mother. Not biological mother, but *Mother*."

An awkward silence followed her statement. "I—"

Thomas took her hand. His touch cut her words off. "We'll both be the parents," he said. Meghan's hand automatically tightened in Thomas's. She refused to look at him. She knew if she did, she wouldn't be able to hold herself together. *Why had he said that?* They were not going to be parents.

"Ideally, when would you like to have the procedure done?" Dr. Petry asked.

Meghan's eyes focused on her. "Two weeks or later," she answered without hesitation, yet she did have to clear her throat. Two weeks would make people think she'd become pregnant during her honeymoon. Even in this day, people still counted to nine when someone was pregnant. Even though the stigma was not transferred to the child, the old standard stood side by side with both tolerance and acceptance.

"So soon," Thomas said. He'd been quiet for most of the discussion. Meghan assumed he'd heard most of it before with his wife. His *first* wife. The words popped into her head without thought. His first wife was dead. *She* was his wife.

Meghan noticed the confused look on the doctor's face, but she asked no questions.

"Is there a reason to wait?" Meghan asked.

"Of course not," Thomas said. "I guess I thought we'd need a little longer."

"Only if Mrs. Worthington-Yates is menstruating. We'll also put you on the necessary hormones and a few tests thereafter so the transfer will be four to six weeks from now."

"I won't be," Meghan told her.

The doctor consulted a calendar on a computer screen and looked back at them.

"I'll put you in six weeks from today," she said. She quickly typed something. "You can talk to the nurse on the way out giving her a few more details." Then she shifted in her chair, turning back to look the two of them in the face. "Your body will need to be prepared for the implantation."

She went on to explain the procedure and what drugs Meghan would need to take to prepare her body for a successful implantation.

"The nurse will explain the medication in more detail and give you the correct dosage."

Meghan nodded.

"Now, I'll need to examine you." She must have pressed a button, for a nurse entered the room. "Mrs. Worthington-Yates, would you come with me, please?"

Meghan got up. She looked at Thomas. He gave her a reassuring nod and she followed the nurse out.

Another point of no return, Meghan thought.

She was pregnant. Meghan hadn't really thought about being pregnant, about the fact of it. It was something off in the unknown and unthought of region of her mind. But as she looked at her body in the mirror, she was sure.

Meghan mentally went through the list of signs the doctor had told her to expect. Not all of them were present, and it was too early for some, but enough were evident to tell her the implantation had worked. To confirm her thought, she bought a pregnancy kit and the pink plus sign came in clear and steady.

Meghan stared at it in her private bathroom. It was hard to believe. Even the confirmation was hard to believe. Miracle baby, Meghan thought. The doctor had given her the term as if she was speaking to a camera crew regarding some unusual phenomenon. This baby, whom Meghan could not see or feel, had defied the odds and taken the first step to becoming a living, breathing human being. He or she was now breathing, so to speak, on her own. Meghan chose to think of it as a girl. She hadn't asked Thomas if he wanted a boy or girl. All she knew was he wanted his and Ruth's child. And it looked as if he was going to have his wish.

Meghan wondered when she would need to go shopping for bigger clothes. The brochures she'd been given on the first nine months said no two pregnancies were alike. She'd discovered that women carried differently based on body structure and how well they stayed in shape. Meghan was in excellent shape due to her exercise program.

The first person a newly pregnant woman should tell was her husband. Meghan left the bathroom and called Dr. Petry. The doctor wanted to see her immediately and Meghan made an appointment for the following day.

It was time to tell Thomas. The two had walked around each other as if the floor would collapse for the last several weeks. Meghan didn't like it. She wanted to at least be friends with him. Being his lover was preferable, but not under the circumstances that he had presented her with. No matter whether she was his lover or only his surrogate, when she left this house her heart would be in jeopardy.

The breakfast room was bright and sunny and faced the back lawn, which was a long, wide vista of emerald-green grass. Off to the side was a pool and a tennis court. Meghan had never seen Thomas play tennis, but he'd begun his day with a swim each morning since they'd been back. She usually swam in the afternoon when the day was hottest. It was refreshing, especially after she'd jogged through the neighborhood. It was this workout that had allowed her to meet some of the neighbors.

If Thomas was still in the house, he would likely be in the breakfast room. Meghan hadn't gone looking for him in a while. Mainly, she avoided him as much as possible. She didn't know what she would say. *Should she just blurt out that she was pregnant? Should she say the process had worked?*

Three steps from the bottom of the staircase Thomas came out of the breakfast room. He wore a light gray suit with a blue shirt and striped tie against glowing skin that still held the sun's effect of their honeymoon. His briefcase was in his right hand. Meghan stopped, her heart thumping like plucked strings on a bass.

"You're up early," Thomas said. His face looked stern.

Meghan wanted him to soften. She wanted to see his eyes filled with desire the way they had been that day in her old house when they'd made love. She wanted to tell him he was going to be a father and have his expression transform into one of pleasure. But she cautioned herself against that possibility. She was supposed to get pregnant. He'd been there for the procedure.

One hand tightened around the banister, the other one held the evidence of her pregnancy.

"Is something wrong?" Thomas asked as silence stretched between them.

"Miracle baby," she said, her voice barely above a whisper.

Thomas's features transformed. Horror showed in his eyes. "What's happened?"

"It worked." She stretched out the hand holding the pregnancy test. "I'm pregnant."

Thomas's gaze bounced back and forth between her face and the small stick in her hand. Fear gripped Meghan's heart. This was not the reaction she wanted or expected.

"It's what you wanted, isn't it?" she asked.

Thomas still hadn't moved or said anything. Then the briefcase in his hand hit the floor. The sound appeared to snap the bonds holding him. Moving with the speed of light, he crossed the floor and grabbed both her and the small stick in her hand.

"Are you sure?" he asked. He glanced at the plus sign. "I mean, you're really sure?"

His arms were around her, holding her, caressing her. His hands moved over her back and into her hair. Meghan was too surprised to do anything. Emotion poured into her bloodstream like scalding water. In a moment, her arms went around him and she clung to him. Everything she wanted on their honeymoon. All the feelings she'd pent up inside her as she'd slept several yards from him burst inside her.

She turned her head, her mouth kissing his neck. His skin was smooth and warm under her mouth. Sensations ripped through her at the feel of him, at being secure in his arms. Thomas took her head and turned it so their lips touched. As if they had both been starving, the touch ignited a spark, which burst into flame. They drank of each other, trading kiss for kiss, arms moving over clothes that impeded their need to touch naked skin.

Exchanging places, her arms circled his neck and his drew her tightly to him. The kiss deepened, passion flared within her and everything around her fell into place. He was everything she wanted. The Thomas she wanted.

Slowly he pushed her back. Meghan was reluctant to end the connection. Together they sat on the steps.

"How are you?" he asked. "Are you all right?"

She was delirious, yet she only nodded. His hand was still around her. He ran it over her stomach and up her side. Meghan felt her breasts tingle in anticipation of him touching them. He didn't. He leaned over and kissed her shoulder, bare except for a tiny strap holding her dress up.

"Should I stay here?"

Her head fell back. She wanted to keep him where he was, wanted him to go on nibbling at her shoulder and to move his mouth further down.

"You can't." Her voice was breathy.

"Why not?"

"You have a business. Meetings."

The word must have registered in his brain. "I do have a meeting, but…" He trailed off.

"It's only the first day." At least the first day that she'd known for sure. "I'll be all right. Plus I have a meeting with the doctor who needs to confirm it."

He got up. Meghan stood, too. He retrieved his briefcase from the place on the floor where it had fallen. Meghan walked him to the door leading to the garage.

"I'll be back tonight." He smiled and kissed her again. Meghan caught his arms and returned it. With another kiss, he went through the door, closing it behind him.

She leaned against the wood, finally feeling like a bride.

Traffic was lighter than Thomas thought it would be. He didn't usually come home every night. He had an apartment in the city and he stayed there most nights. Since Meghan had moved in, he'd wanted to see her. Even though he told himself he didn't, he knew now that was a lie.

He'd proved it to himself, when she said she was pregnant. Stunned for a moment, his reaction was spontaneous. He'd gone forward to look at the pregnancy test she was holding, but found her in his arms. When her mouth touched his neck, it was his undoing. He let it all go, took her mouth as if doing so would save his life.

He wanted her, all of her. He wanted to make love as long and hard as he could, but she was pregnant and that saved him from carrying her up those steps and spending the day in bed, his meetings be damned.

Checking his watch, Thomas had another hour before getting to his office. He wasn't going to make it in time for the meeting. Calling his secretary, he had the meeting moved back one hour. He'd need time once he got there to prepare his mind, which was focused on Meghan, before sitting before a roomful of investment analysts and talking about stock quotes and futures.

When he hung up from the office, he hit the speed-dial number for Nina and Adam.

"Thomas, what a surprise." Adam answered on the second ring.

"Good morning, Adam."

"How that's pretty little bride of yours?"

Thomas took a deep breath. He was under no illusion that his father-in-law thought it was time for him to move on. Even though Thomas had been married to his daughter, Adam Russell thought it was time for him to find someone else to share his life. Thomas had. He would be sharing it with his son or daughter.

"Adam, I called to let you and Nina know that Meghan is pregnant. The miracle happened."

Adam stuttered. "Are…are you sure? Are you really sure?"

"She had a pregnancy test. It was positive." Thomas laughed at the evident happiness in his father-in-law's voice.

"I can't wait to tell Nina. She'll be so happy."

"She isn't there?"

"She went to have her hair done. I don't know why. Her hair looked fine to me. But you know women."

An image of Meghan jumped into his head. Her hair was beautiful. It was soft to the touch and always smelled clean. He could still smell the scent of her. A car horn blared behind him and Thomas jerked back into his lane.

"Thomas, you okay?"

"Yeah, Adam. Just got a little distracted."

"Well, I won't hold you. I want to call Nina and let her in on the good news."

"Give her my love," Thomas said and punched the button to disconnect the call.

He could imagine Nina's eyes lighting up when Adam called her. She might just forget to dry her hair and walk out with it wet and in rollers. He smiled at the thought. Nina would be just as happy as Adam had been when Meghan had told him. Only his happiness was confused, mingled with the woman he'd held in his arms less than an hour ago and his dead wife.

Chapter 11

The Thomas Worthington-Yates who came home that night was not the same man who had kissed her to distraction that morning. Somewhere along the line he changed to someone else. He wasn't the polite stranger he'd been for the last few weeks, but he wasn't the human being Meghan knew he could be.

And she wanted that human being.

"Thomas, what happened today?"

"You mean at the office?"

"No. I mean to you."

They were sitting at the dinner table, eating a meal that she had cooked. She'd taken special care to prepare a nice dinner. There were flowers on the table, but they were always there, so he wouldn't think anything of them. Her dress was new, something she'd bought with

Nina before the wedding, but had not worn until today. Yet Thomas was distracted. She could have been wearing a bathrobe and eating Chinese take-out.

"What do you mean, me?"

"You're different. This morning—"

"I don't want to talk about this morning."

"It was a mistake?" She braced herself for a positive response, but he said nothing, leaving her even more confused.

Meghan swallowed. "I don't want to go back to yesterday."

He looked at her. "What are you talking about?"

"I'm talking about the way you tiptoe around me. The way I tiptoe around you."

"I don't—"

"Don't deny it," she said. "You move around as if I'm not here, speaking to me only when necessary, spending as much time away from me as possible. If you want me to go, I can find my apartment now and move in. You don't have to see me again. I'm sure they'll transfer the baby to you at the hospital."

Meghan got up and walked from the room. She headed upstairs to pack. She was sure she could stay with Evelyn until she found a place of her own. If she was lucky, maybe the house she'd vacated would still be available.

"Meghan," Thomas called her name.

She didn't stop walking. She'd had all she was going to take.

"Wait," he said. Meghan kept going. Thomas caught up with her at the top of the stairs. Meghan stopped when he put his hand on her arm. Thomas dropped it almost immediately as if her skin was hot. Maybe she'd burned his hand, she thought snidely.

The hallway was wide, wider than in most houses. For the first time Meghan wondered if he'd had it built to certain specifications. There was a padded bench against a near wall. Farther down was a table with a light on it that came on and went off automatically.

"Let's sit down."

Thomas moved and Meghan went with him. They sat on the soft fabric that had probably seen few visitors.

Thomas leaned forward, his arms on his legs, his hands folded between them.

"It's hard to talk about," he started.

Meghan waited. She could probably help him, but she was feeling too much like the victim. He could explain his behavior on his own.

"I know I appear to be moody. To change from day to day."

"Why is that?"

"I just have a lot on my mind."

"Maybe telling me about it could help."

He shook his head.

"Unless I'm part of the problem."

Thomas turned toward her, looking her directly in the eye. "You are." Meghan couldn't get angry over his statement. He'd spoken so softly that it sounded like a prayer. He stared at her for a long moment. "I don't mean you're a problem. I'm the problem."

"This is about Ruth." Meghan stated it as fact.

He nodded.

She knew she shouldn't do this, but her training was too ingrained. It was her job to give options, to point out the obvious, list the pathways that certain decisions could lead to. Thomas was in pain. She could see that. More than the social worker in her wanted to relieve it. She was falling for him and it didn't matter that he was still in love with his first wife, Meghan hated to see him in turmoil.

"I'll make this easy for you," she said.

He frowned at her.

"We don't go back to yesterday."

He nodded, waiting for her to continue.

"And we don't go to this morning, either."

"Where do we go?" he asked as if yesterday and this morning were the only options.

"We become friends. Good friends. We're open and honest with each other. We don't avoid each other. We don't tiptoe around each other. And there are no strings." That also meant no lovemaking, no intimate touching, no kissing. "If I stick to my routine and you to yours, when this is over neither of us will be any the worse for wear." She waited a moment for her words to sink in.

"In other words, we go back to the original agreement?"

She nodded. "Do you think you can do that?"

"I don't know. Do you think you can?"

She knew he was remembering that morning. The kiss on the stairs had been life-altering. Making love had been a no-holds-barred roller coaster that took her to the top of the world.

"We can try," Meghan finally said.

"And if it doesn't work?"

She opened her eyes wide. "We go to Plan B."

And thus began their new routine. Meghan came down for breakfast with Thomas on days he was home. When he wasn't going to be home, he always called. In the evening he would tell her about his day. Meghan listened attentively. She loved hearing his voice. It was dark and rich and she imagined hearing it in the dark of her room.

Meghan spent her days jogging or taking walks, reading about pregnancy on the Internet and checking books out of the local library. There were days when she cooked the evening meal, but for the most part she was bored. Used to being active, she didn't understand how people sat around all day with nothing to do. A few of the neighbors she'd met invited her to lunch or shopping.

Two months after Dr. Petry confirmed her pregnancy, Meghan began to tire easily and took frequent naps.

"What did you do today?" Thomas asked after they'd cleared away the dinner dishes. With Meghan in the house, Mrs. Barrie enjoyed leaving early.

"Evelyn came out and had lunch with me."

"How is she?" Thomas smiled. "I like her. I wish she'd stayed for dinner."

"She got a job doing makeup for the actors at the Everyman Theatre and had to get back early. She said she hoped to see you next time."

He smiled.

Meghan yawned.

"Are you tired?"

"A little," she said. "It's normal, according to what I've read. I take a nap in the afternoon."

"Do you feel all right?"

"I feel fine. Now tell me, how was your day?"

"It was good. We got a new client. Well, almost one. I'll have to go to San Antonio in a week to finalize the details."

Meghan felt as if a part of her had been torn away. "How long will you be gone?" she asked.

"Three or four days."

He was often away that long, staying in the city instead of making the long drive every day, but somehow two thousand miles seemed like the end of the earth.

"Will you be all right here alone? I can ask Mrs. Barrie to stay the night."

"She doesn't stay when you go to your apartment."

"I know, but I'd feel more comfortable knowing you weren't alone."

"Would you take me with you?" The words were out before she could call them back. Thomas stared at her. "I know it's an imposition. I just thought…"

"Do you really want to go?"

"I've never been to San Antonio."

"What about the baby?"

That would be his first concern, Meghan thought. "I'm only two months pregnant. I have no medical restrictions."

"I just thought…traveling…" He hesitated.

Meghan remembered that Ruth had died in a car accident. Thomas was probably thinking that she could die the same way.

"I won't be driving."

"That doesn't matter. Are you sure you want to go?"

"I won't interfere in your business. And I can entertain myself."

"I'll have the tickets ordered," he said.

Meghan nearly threw herself into his arms. At the last minute she remembered to keep her hands to herself.

San Antonio was hot, dusty and monochromatic. Thomas spent most of the day and part of the night in meetings. He came in exhausted. Meghan was on her own most of the time. She toured the famous Alamo and surrounding area, but found being away from Baltimore was just as boring as staying alone in the house.

Looking out of the hotel window, Meghan saw the dusty landscape fanning to the horizon. Below her was the pool. The water was crystal clear and looked inviting.

Twenty minutes later she was swimming laps. She swam until she was tired, then took one of the lawn chairs and sat in the hot, dry air. She hadn't intended to fall asleep, but the exercise and her pregnancy conspired against her. Her eyelids drooped and she fell into a dreamless sleep.

"Mrs. Worthington-Yates?"

Meghan thought she heard her name three times before she opened her eyes. She was not used to being called by Thomas's last name. Her name was Meghan Howard, but to the world she was now Mrs. Worthington-Yates.

"You've been asleep for half an hour. The sun can really burn you out here." A pool attendant spoke to her, a short Latina woman with an armload of towels.

"Oh, I didn't intend to fall asleep. Thank you for

waking me." Meghan sat up and cried out in pain. Instinctively, her hand went to her arm, but touching herself only caused more pain.

"Here," the attendance said, handing her a tube of aloe. "Don't shower. The spray will sting. Take a cool bath and put this on the burns afterwards. It'll take the sting out. You'll be all right in a couple of days."

Meghan struggled to her feet and gingerly walked to the elevator and back to her room. Seeing her reflection in the mirror had her making a horrible face. She looked as if she was wearing a mask. Her sunglasses had covered her eyes and prevented the sun from deepening the color over that part of her face. Her nose was Rudolph-red. Her arms and legs that hadn't been covered by her one-piece bathing suit had darkened to burnt gold.

No way could she hide this from Thomas. When he got in, she was usually asleep, but she always got up to have breakfast with him. If she didn't show up in the morning, he'd come investigating. His first concern would be for the baby, so he'd make sure she was all right before going out. She didn't think she'd hurt the baby. Millions of women got sunburned and she'd never heard anything about that having an effect on the fetus.

She ran water in the bathtub and slipped down into it. The soft cloths provided by the hotel were too rough for her skin.

"Stupid," she told herself as she soaped the cloth and used it to drop water on her body. Using the same method, she rinsed herself and softly pressed the plush towels on her wet skin until it was only slightly damp. Air dried the rest of her.

Then she slipped into a long-sleeved blouse she'd brought because the air conditioner might be too cold and a pair of long cotton pants. Most of her was covered either with cloth or makeup when Thomas came in earlier than expected.

"Meghan?" Thomas called her name. She jerked at the unexpectedness of hearing him. Tiny soldiers with bayonets stabbed her arms and legs. She bit back the scream that jumped into her throat.

Another step and he'd see her. She'd done what the attendant told her to do, but she hadn't added any makeup to her face, only some creams and lotions.

"I thought we could go—" He stopped as soon as she swung her head to look at her. "What happened?"

In one step, he was beside her. He bent down to inspect her face.

"I fell asleep in the sun," she admitted. "I know I look like I'm wearing a mask."

He laughed. "You do at that."

Meghan would have swiped her hand at him, if she wasn't aware that the action would cause pain in her arm. "If the attendant hadn't wakened me, I'd probably need medical care."

"This isn't permanent?" He pulled an empty chair up next to her and sat down.

She shook her head. "In a couple of days I'll be back to normal. At least that's what the attendant said." She paused. "You were saying something when you came in."

"Oh, I thought we'd stay two extra days, go out tonight, have dinner, do some sightseeing. You should really see the city and I know I've left you alone since we arrived."

"Does this mean you've completed your business?"

"All done. I can relax for a couple of days."

He was practically oozing happiness. "And it worked out well?"

"Better than well." He leaned toward her. The chair he'd pulled up was close enough for their knees to touch, but Meghan's were under the desk, safely protected by loose-fitting pants. "We got the contract with all the conditions my legal staff said we needed."

"Congratulations." She reached for his arm, but stopped before touching him. "This will be a celebration?"

"Yes, we're going to go out with another couple."

"I didn't think any of the others had brought their spouses." She could have had company on her solitary trips. If only she'd known one of the other wives was in the hotel.

"They didn't. Bill Stone's wife is flying in today. The others are going home tonight."

"Bill? He's one of the lawyers, right?"

"Right."

"What time is dinner?"

"We're meeting them at seven downstairs."

"I'll be ready." Meghan smiled but wondered if she'd be able to walk with the sunburn.

"Bill's wife's name is Donna. The two of you will have something in common."

"What's that?"

"She's pregnant with their third child. Three or four months, I believe."

"Do they know I'm pregnant? I mean, have you told the people at your office?"

Thomas shook his head. "Not yet."

"Being cautious?"

"Maybe. I've been through this several times and I don't want to announce anything and then have something go wrong."

"Thomas, nothing is going to go wrong. This is the miracle baby." She smiled and he did, too. Meghan wanted to touch him. She clasped her hands to keep from doing it. "I'm healthy and in reasonably good shape. I'm taking all of my vitamins and getting plenty of exercise."

"I know. But up until the end of the second trimester you're still at risk to miscarry."

"I'll be careful," she said.

Thomas reached over and took one of her hands. She swung around in the chair and he took the other one. It was the first time he'd touched her in a long time. While most of her body was sunburned, her hands had been protected by the towel she'd used to dry off after her swim. She'd draped it across her midsection. Yet her hands trembled when Thomas folded them in his larger ones.

They both stared at their entwined fingers. Meghan felt the heat of his fingertips climbing up her arms and doing battle with the bayonet soldiers for dominance along her skin. Thomas's assault forces won. Meghan lifted her eyes. Thomas's gaze bore deeply into hers. She saw desire there. Her body suffused with need for him.

She felt the electricity that always accompanied his presence kick up a few kilowatts. The room seemed dim. Meghan didn't know if it was cloud covering the sun outside or her eyelids dropping that blocked out the light. Her body searched for something to ground the power of Thomas's attraction, but found nothing. She leaned forward, unable and unwilling to stop herself. She wanted him, craved his touch, hungered to feel his body against hers just once more.

Her chair creaked. The effect was that of a pin bursting the balloon that had blown up around them, enveloping them in a world of rapture. Meghan's eyes snapped wide and she pushed back. At the same time, Thomas dropped his hold on her hands and moved away, too.

He stood up, stepping away from her. "I'm going to shower," he said.

Too much information, Meghan thought. Directly after she'd leaned in to kiss him, he presented her with an image of his naked body, wet and hard.

This arrangement was not working. Cool water sluiced over Thomas's neck and shoulders, but it didn't calm his rapidly beating heart or the fact that he wanted to take her to bed and keep her there for as long as he was physically able.

Ruth had stood between them. Thomas had sworn he'd never fall in love again and he was not admitting that the loved Meghan now, but he wanted her. More than he'd wanted the other women in his life. He knew he could fall in love in this one.

And now there was a baby. Not their baby, but his and Ruth's. He poured shampoo on his hair and thought about how he'd gotten into this situation. He was sure it would be a contractual situation, like the one he'd just completed. But this was Meghan and the contract was missing one thing—the arm's-length transaction. She wasn't an arm's length away. He didn't want her that far. He wanted her inside his arms. It didn't matter that she slept more than an arm's length from him. It didn't matter than he'd spent this entire trip at meetings avoiding her. She distracted him just by being alive. She entered his dreams and popped into his head at odd moments.

He'd lift a cup of coffee and remember her drinking decaf during one of their evening talks. He'd see a woman in shorts and remember Meghan's long legs in her jogging pants. At night when he returned to the suite, he couldn't resist checking to see if she was all right.

But where did that leave him and Ruth? And what about the child? Meghan was pregnant. There was another life to consider. And Meghan had told him re-negotiation wasn't something she was open to.

Thomas had rarely been in this position before. He usually got his way. But never had he dealt in human flesh. Switching off the taps, he stepped from the shower and wrapped his body in a towel.

Stepping into the bedroom, he had no doubt that he wanted to deal in Meghan's flesh.

When he came out of the bedroom forty minutes later, he'd shaved and dressed. Meghan sat on a barstool at the counter. She slipped off of it and faced him when she heard the click of his door. Thomas let out a long slow breath.

"Wow," he said. He'd said it the first time she'd bowled him over and each time since. She wore a long, floral dress that had only tantalized him in his want to slip his hands across it and around her slight body.

"Wow," Meghan answered. It had become their

greeting, but Thomas meant it. The lighting suited her, casting a soft glow on her newly tanned face. Her feet were bare, showing unpainted toenails. Hair with reddish highlights glowed about her face like a frame.

"What did you do to your face?"

"Makeup," she said. "I hope it isn't too much."

Thomas walked to her. He stopped barely a foot away. He noticed her breathing, the rising and falling of her breasts. It seemed a little shallow, as if she were intentionally trying to control it.

"No," he said. "It's perfect."

They looked into each other's eyes for a moment. Thomas was in danger of catching her to him. "Shoes?" he asked.

"What?"

"Aren't you going to wear shoes?"

She looked down, wiggled her toes and looked back at him.

"My feet are much more comfortable without them," she said. Then she slipped them into the sandals sitting by the barstool. Thomas wished he'd declined dinner with Bill and Donna. He'd much rather spend it alone with Meghan, even though he knew how dangerous that could be.

Chapter 12

Eliza Doolittle had nothing on Meghan Worthington-Yates. Meghan could have danced all night, too. Bill and Donna Stone were a wonderful couple. Meghan enjoyed talking to her. Bill was a lawyer and Donna, in addition to mothering two children and carrying the third, was a dentist with a lucrative practice in Baltimore.

But despite their engaging conversation, the evening was capped by her dancing with Thomas. Being in his arms with the music surrounding them was like heaven. She only slightly felt the effects of her afternoon in the sun. Maybe she would pay for it later, but she didn't care. She got to be in his arms, to close her eyes and feel him, smell his unique scent.

She hummed as they got off the elevator and Thomas opened the door to the now dark suite. Meghan stopped short and stepped out of her shoes. Thomas walked into her. His arm instinctively came out to save her from toppling forward.

Meghan could not stop the cry of pain that shot through her arms when his arms pulled her against him.

"Are you all right?" Thomas asked, but he didn't release her.

Meghan nodded. He turned her into his arms. Meghan winced, but kept her head low so he couldn't see her face.

"I can't live like this, Meghan," Thomas said. "You're driving me crazy."

He lifted her face then, saw the look in her eyes. Meghan couldn't have disguised it if she wanted to. All those times they'd walked on eggshells had been to keep from breaking the fragile membrane separating them. Meghan knew she should step back. She should move out of his arms and escape to the safety of her bedroom. But his eyes were holding her. She couldn't move, didn't want to be anywhere other than where she was.

Meghan moved first, but Thomas met her. Crushing her to him, his mouth was hard as it took hers. She tasted the sweetness of the wine he'd drank at dinner. His arms tightened around her. But lying still wasn't something she could do. His mouth tantalized hers. She trembled in his arms. Her arms lifted, searching, finding and circling his neck. She pressed into him, her fingers caressing the nape of his neck as his mouth forced her head back.

His hands moved around her back, his fingers drawing downward from her breasts to her hips. Thomas cupped her bottom and pulled her into him. Meghan settled her body into his as if they were two halves of the same whole.

His lips slipped from her mouth to her neck. Meghan's head fell back, giving Thomas greater access, relishing the flood of pleasure that threatened to overwhelm her.

Meghan's heart raced. Her senses threatened to overload. She felt like fire, sure that combustion would take place at any moment.

Thomas's hand found the zipper on her dress and she felt the air on her back as he pulled it down. Meghan breathed heavily. Anticipation and passion vied for control. His head lifted and he looked into her eyes. Then his mouth repositioned on hers. He squeezed her to him, drawing her shoulders close. The dress fell off her shoulders, passing her fingers. Without a sound, it fell to the floor.

Thomas looked at her. Meghan felt no modesty under his gaze. He kissed her shoulder, roughly. Meghan winced at his touch. Thomas stopped. He stepped back, looking at her. Suddenly everything changed.

"Ruth, what have you done?"

Meghan went cold. Her body froze. She couldn't move, couldn't speak. Her body was numb. Where things had been hot, they were now icy, frigid. Meghan felt naked. She wanted to put her hands up and protect her, run from Thomas's eyes.

She took two steps back, each one out of the dress that lay at her feet. She didn't look down, but kept her gaze steady on the man in front of her.

"Meghan," she said, her voice no lower than a soft whisper. "Meghan. Not Ruth."

She was avoiding him. And rightly so. All the ground he and Meghan had gained was lost with a single word.

It hadn't been intentional. Then it never is in those situations. Thomas looked at the photo of Ruth on his desk.

"You knew this wouldn't work from the beginning, didn't you?" he asked the immobile figure. Ruth smiled at him, unchanging. She wasn't there to answer his questions, to help him through situations the way she had done in the past. He loved her. He'd always love her. But now there was Meghan. And Thomas knew Meghan had melted the ice around his heart.

He no longer stayed in Baltimore overnight. He made the trip home every night in hopes of being with her. He'd been doing it for nearly three weeks. Meghan was polite, but she went no further toward being friendly.

Thomas missed talking to her. Their after-dinner conversations came to an abrupt halt after San Antonio. Meghan accepted his apology, but went back to being a guest in his house. She didn't keep to her rooms. He knew she swam and went for walks. She shopped with Mrs. Barrie and had lunch with some of the neighbors, people Thomas hadn't met in all the years he'd owned the house. Often he could hear her laughing in the kitchen or enjoying a television comedy. When he came in, she would change. All the laughter went out of her and she'd find she needed to do something in another part of the house.

He felt left out, as if this was her home and he was the unwelcome guest. When he glimpsed at Meghan he could see the changes in her body. Her stomach bulged slightly. She hadn't begun wearing maternity clothes, but her wardrobe had changed to loosely fitting dresses.

Thomas wanted so to go back to that room in San

Antonio. He wanted to take back the word he'd said. He wanted to go back to being her friend. He was ready to accept that.

He lifted the photo of Ruth. "I love you, Ruth," he told her. "I will always love you."

Then he put the photo in the drawer. For the first time since Ruth died, he knew he had to live. And he was going to do everything he could to make Meghan part of that life.

And he was going to start today.

Leaving the office, he drove through the rain. It didn't let up all the way home.

"Meghan?" he called as he came through the door. She didn't answer. He went through the downstairs rooms looking for her. In the kitchen Mrs. Barrie told him Meghan was in the gym.

Thomas pulled his tie loose and took off his jacket. Leaving them with his briefcase on a chair by the stairs, he took the stairs two and three at a time.

"Meghan," he called, opening the door. He stopped when he saw her. She was sweating as she ran on the treadmill. "What are you doing?" he shouted over the noise.

She turned the machine off. "I believe we've already played this scene."

She moved to step around him, but Thomas blocked her way.

"That came out wrong. I just thought running wouldn't be good for—"

"The baby?" Anger laced her question. "Thomas, I'm fine. The baby is fine. I'm not doing anything that hurts. The doctor says I can continue doing anything I did before unless it hurts."

"I was going to say *you*."

He watched the fight go out of her. She looked lost, like a language was being spoken that she'd never heard.

"I thought pregnant women could easily lose their balance."

"That's in the last trimester. It's more being clumsy than balance," she said. "At least that's what the books say."

"Do you think we could talk for a minute?"

"Sure," she sat down on the floor, cross-legged.

Thomas hadn't sat like that in years, but he lowered himself down and sat in front of her.

"Ruth was impulsive at times. She would do things without thinking about the consequences. She wasn't reckless, but there were things that she didn't think about. I loved her for some of those impulses."

Meghan watched him without speaking. Her eyes were wide, fringed with long lashes that he hoped the child would inherit if it was a girl. He shook his head to clear it. *How could he have made that leap?* He was talking about Ruth. The child was Ruth's, not Meghan's. Ruth's eye lashes weren't nearly as long as Meghan's. He'd called Meghan Ruth and now he was confusing Ruth with Meghan.

"That night in San Antonio, when I saw the sunburn, it was something Ruth would have done. Forgetting about sunscreen, falling asleep in the sun. My reaction was instinctive, but I didn't mean to call you by her name." He paused a moment, hoping she was believing him. "I want to recapture your friendship."

"You think you've lost it?"

He nodded. "I do. You avoid me. When I come into a room, you leave. It's pretty evident you don't care to be in my presence."

She didn't deny it. "That's not the reason," she finally said.

"What is the reason?"

"Something has…was happening that was wrong."

"Wrong? What?"

"Me, I was wrong. I set the rules and I wasn't following them."

"You mean the kiss?"

She nodded.

"I was on the other side of it and it appeared mutual. I have no regrets. I'd do it again in a heartbeat."

He searched Meghan's face for her reaction. He didn't know what to make of it. He wanted to find acceptance there. She blushed, but he didn't know what to make of that, either.

"That's not how it works," she told him. "We don't come from the same world. When this is over, we go back to being who we were."

"We'll never go back to being that," he said.

She looked surprised. "What do you mean?"

Thomas moved a little closer to her. "It's like seeing the future." He used his hand to create a window. "If you could, it wouldn't be the future."

"Why not?"

"Because you looked at it. You would change it."

"You're saying I've changed my future."

He nodded. "And I've changed mine."

"And by us being friends, we're going into a philosophical discussion on what the future holds?"

He laughed. "Only if you want to. I'm saying things don't have to be the way we think they have to be. We have the ability to change them."

"What do you want to change?"

"I don't know. I just know when we used to talk in the evenings, I liked it. I was happy. When we stopped, after San Antonio, I felt as if I'd lost something. Something good. I enjoyed talking about my day and hearing about yours. It made me happy. I want to go back to that time."

"I don't think anyone has ever said that to me. That I make them happy."

"Well, I just did and you do."

"What a wonderful husband." Meghan overheard two women talking in the dressing room. "My husband wouldn't be caught in the parking lot of a place like this."

"Try this one," Thomas said.

Meghan turned and smiled at him. She took the red outfit he held. Thomas was true to his word. He left the office in time to get home for dinner every night. They talked and ate and spent the evening in each other's company. Some days she went into the city and stayed in his apartment. They went to the theater, had lunch with Evelyn and visited with Mr. Forrest from the old neighborhood.

In every way but one, he was her husband. And now he was in a maternity shop with her helping to choose outfits. It was her fourth month and Meghan could no longer fit into her clothes.

Meghan's stomach was growing steadily. For a long time there'd been no evidence of her pregnancy, then suddenly she bulged. Since then it was a few pounds a month. The doctor, however, was happy with her weight.

Meghan put the dress up to her and looked at it and then at Thomas.

"It looks great. Try it on."

She headed toward the dressing room, when she suddenly stopped. "Oh," she said, grabbing her stomach. The clothes in her hands fell to the floor.

"What?" Thomas dropped what he held and rushed to her. "What's wrong?" He put his hand on her back and her arm as if she needed support.

She looked at him. For no reason at all, tears filled her eyes.

"What's wrong?" he asked again.

A small crowd gathered around her, including the two women from the dressing room.

"I think I was just kicked."

An audible sigh of relief came from all around her, all except Thomas. His face was still a mask of concern.

It happened again. Meghan bit her lip to stop crying out. The feeling was surprising. She never expected anything to feel as if it was knocking on her stomach from the inside. Grabbing Thomas's hand, Meghan placed it on her stomach.

The baby kicked again. She smiled. Thomas spontaneously turned her into his arms and hugged her.

Much about him had changed since their talk on the gym floor. Meghan wondered about what he'd said. Did they have a future together? Was that what he was trying to say? Or was it just that they'd come to a crossroads in their lives and when she delivered and left, the road she would take wasn't going back to the life she'd known but to a different future?

At that moment, Meghan didn't care. She held Thomas's hand while they shared in the tiny miracle that was a baby.

It didn't take long for the baby to go from cute little kicks to somersaults. And she seemed to love to do them after Meghan went to bed. At six months Meghan felt like a whale. And there was another trimester to go.

Meghan turned over, her girth weighting her so that once she was in the roll she couldn't stop herself from falling on her back. Finding a comfortable position in which to sleep was like looking for extraterrestrial life. When she did get a few moments of rest, the baby began to kick again and woke her. *Did they all kick so hard during the night? How did it know she was trying to sleep?*

She breathed hard. This position was laboring. She had to force more air into her lungs. She turned again. This time toward the side of her bed that was easier to get out. Although with only three months to term, she found getting out of bed a challenge. Her body no longer bent at the waist. Since there was no waist, that must be the reason.

Grabbing the headboard, she hoisted herself into a half-sitting position. Then she turned on her side and swung her feet over the side and leveraged herself into a full stand.

"Whew," she said.

Donning her robe, she left the bedroom, walking barefoot to the steps and down them to the kitchen. She got a glass of milk and drank it, then went into the room she thought of as the conservatory. Thomas, no doubt, would disagree with this designation. The room had a grand piano as the focal point. There was a stereo system hidden in a closed cabinet, along with an eclectic collection of music. She discovered from her nighttime tours that Thomas liked rock and roll classics, jazz and show tunes. Ruth must have liked the easy-listening collection. Some of the CD cases had her name printed on them.

Meghan didn't consider herself as having a specific taste. She liked what she liked. A lot of it depended on the time of her life, what struck her as relevant.

Using a remote, she selected a collection from the classic rock era. A group called the Brooklyn Bridge began to sing. She recognized the song if not this rendition of it.

A book she'd left earlier sat on an end table next to the sofa. Sitting down, she picked it up. Maybe reading would make her sleepy and she'd be able to get some rest before she heard Thomas coming down for breakfast and then leaving for the office.

She read, but retained none of the story. As the CD ended, Meghan put aside her book and walked to the piano. Sitting on the padded bench, she raised the cover over the keys. They were gleaming white. She rubbed her fingers across them, but depressed none of them and the instrument made no sound. Meghan liked pianos, loved hearing someone play, but she didn't play herself.

There was a time she wanted to learn, but there had been no piano or money for lessons in her childhood.

She had learned a few things in school when other people showed her how to finger some of the chords. She'd even been able to pick out some popular songs on Mr. Forrest's piano while visiting after school, or during holiday get-togethers.

She didn't try to remember any of them now. Her hands hit a few notes and the sound tinkled into the room.

She smiled, wondering about people who could make this instrument talk to them, produce glorious messages that calmed or incited or spurred memory, relaxed or made them get up and dance. It was a power and a gift.

She pressed more keys, remembering the chords she knew and using them. No particular song was recognizable, but she enjoyed hearing the soft notes.

A kick came again. Not as hard as the one that had awakened her.

"What's wrong, don't you like the music?" she asked the baby. Unfortunately, she never answered.

Meghan went back to the music, concentrating on her limited skill. After a moment she felt a presence and looked up. Thomas stood in the doorway. He leaned against the doorjamb dressed in a long silk robe. The sash was loosely tied and she could see bare skin from his neck to his waist. She wondered if he was wearing anything beneath it. Her body suddenly flashed hot. Even in pregnancy, sexual arousal was still evident.

"How long have you been standing there?" she asked.

Before he answered, she got the hardest kick to

date. It had her bellow in pain. Thomas was at her side in an instant.

"What's wrong?" His hand covered hers without either of them thinking about it.

"This gymnast of yours is trying to get out, but she isn't going through the right channels." She smiled. The pain was subsiding.

"I'm sorry," Thomas apologized.

"Don't be." She took the hand on her belly and moved it. "Here." She placed it on the spot where he kicked. Several thumps beat against his hand.

"Feels like he's ready."

"Especially at night," she agreed. "And it's a girl."

"Does he keep you awake?" he said, ignoring her.

"Sometimes." She didn't tell him that she prowled the house most nights. Thankfully, she was able to take naps during the day. With him out and Mrs. Barrie busy, Meghan had ample time to try to recover her sleep. The only problem was, she never could stay asleep long.

"Is that normal?"

"According to my group of surrogates, it's very normal. Sometimes I come in here and lie on the sofa. It helps to have something solid against my back. Not to mention, it's easier to get up since I can no longer bend."

He eyed her for a long moment. His expression was thoughtful, but she could see it also contained a little pain.

"Do you regret any of this?"

Meghan got up then. His hand was still on her stomach. She needed to remove it and this was the more genteel way.

"I'll probably regret stretch marks and not being able to sleep, and…"

"You won't have stretch marks," he interrupted. "You have the kind of skin that doesn't mar easily."

Meghan was knocked off her usual keel. He'd taken the time to notice her skin. That was surprising and caused a low humming in her ears. What a surprising man, she thought. He was a wizard, an investments expert. Meghan never thought he'd notice her outside those times it was necessary, but to take in small details about her was more than interesting.

Thomas left the piano bench and came to sit across from her. "So you play?" he asked.

She glanced at the piano. "I wish I could. Do you play?"

"A little. The piano was Ruth's favorite. She was very good."

"Tell me about her. There are no photos that I've seen. You say very little about her and you obviously had a loving marriage."

He was silent for a long time. "That's a hard question to answer. How do you sum up a person's life in a few sentences?"

Meghan started to say they had time, but she remembered Thomas had to work in the morning.

"She was happy, fun, laughed easily. At school she was an art major. She wanted to be a designer, have her own line."

"Clothes?"

"Furniture. She loved antiques, but her designs fell more into the contemporary arena."

"Did she ever do it?"

He shook his head. "She had some designs accepted by manufacturers in North Carolina and a couple in China, but then she took ill."

Meghan watched him carefully as he spoke. He stopped, probably remembering the battle she'd waged and lost.

"She loved children. She and I were both only children. It was our intention to have a houseful of kids, but nature had a different plan."

"How did you decide on a surrogate?"

"That was Nina's idea. She'd read something about frozen embryos and researched it. Ruth jumped at the idea. She wanted her own child more than anything."

"What about you?"

Meghan knew she was doing the right thing, but she wanted to reinforce the idea.

"At first I wasn't an enthusiast, but then something happened that changed my mind. I found I was nearly obsessed with wanting my own child."

"What was the something?"

Thomas didn't answer. After a while Meghan knew he wasn't going to. She didn't press him. She stretched out on the sofa, with her back to the cushions, and drew her feet up under her robe.

Her eyes closed and she relaxed.

"Come on," Thomas said.

Opening her eyes, she saw him standing in front of her, his hand extended to help her rise.

"You go on," she said. "I think I'll sleep here." Meghan yawned, her eyes closing. "The sofa back is more comfortable than the bed anyway."

The lamp on the side table went out.

"Thank you," she muttered, snuggling into position.

Her eyes flew open when she felt Thomas slip his hands under her and lift her off the sofa.

"What are you doing?" she asked.

He walked into the hallway. "I'm taking you upstairs."

"But…"

"I'll put something solid against your back. The sofa is no place to sleep."

At the steps he lowered her to the floor. Holding her hand, he led her upstairs.

"Why did you put me down?" she asked. "I thought you were going to carry me to my room."

"I won't take the chance of falling and hurting all three of us."

Meghan smiled, but she knew he was being cautious for the baby. They'd come this far with the miracle child. No need to intentionally set up a hazardous situation.

At the top of the steps he lifted her again.

"Surprised?" he asked.

"I thought I was the one with the surprises."

"You are, but I'm allowed a small quota."

She was to find that out immediately. Instead of him taking her to her room, he eased the door of his own wider and went inside with her in his arms.

Thomas laid Meghan on the bed. He drew the covers up over her.

"Thomas?" she asked questioningly.

"You'll be comfortable here," he said. "I'll be the something solid behind your back."

Meghan's eyes showed panic. She tried to sit up. Thomas reached out and pushed her down.

"I'm fine, Thomas. I can sleep in my own room and I won't wander around at night."

"Stay where you are," he told her, intentionally keeping his voice level and even. He knew her being in his bed was going to be hard for him, but he wanted her comfortable. "Try to relax. Go to sleep."

Meghan closed her eyes, but Thomas could tell from the tenseness in her body that she wouldn't sleep until she relaxed.

He didn't try to get her to do it. He switched off the lights and slipped into bed with her. Meghan moved slightly away from him. He touched her, prepared for her to react. Her body quivered under his touch.

"Relax," he whispered. As she did, he moved closer until he was directly behind her, a sofa for her back. But his body also reacted to her nearness. Holding himself in check, he prayed that he'd have enough endurance to maintain it until she fell asleep.

Chapter 13

"I don't see why we need to do this today," Nina said. "There's plenty of time for you to find an apartment."

"Nina, I'm in my seventh month. I'm going to need someplace to go when the baby is born."

"You act like Thomas is going to throw you out on the street the moment you deliver. You can stay for several months. He's used to you. The baby will need you."

"Nina." The warning note in Meghan's voice showed her frustration. "We both know that's not true."

The car stopped in front of a building on River Street. The neighborhood was clean and the buildings well maintained. Meghan liked it. Getting out of the car, they went inside. Meghan was comfortable with Thomas. She was sleeping in his bed every night, his arms around her, comforting her back. She could easily spend her life there.

But that wasn't the plan.

The manager met them inside the door. They took the elevator to the tenth floor and he showed them the apartment. It was spacious—two bedrooms, large closets, a newly remodeled kitchen, carpeting throughout, but Nina found something wrong with it.

It was too bright or too dark. The carpet was the wrong color. Her furniture wouldn't look good with it. Nina had never seen Meghan's furniture, but that didn't stop her. She was almost funny. Meghan loved her and understood her motives, but she couldn't buy into them.

"I really like this one," Meghan said, stepping into the second bedroom. "I can make this one both a bedroom and office. It'll be a great place to study once I go back to school."

"You haven't even decided where you're going to school. Maybe you should move after you have everything in order."

"Nina, I know what you're trying to do." Nina looked innocent as if she had no idea what Meghan was talking about. "It won't work. Thomas is not in love with me."

"But you're in love with him."

Meghan stopped. Slowly she turned to look at her friend. "I've known it for a long time, so you don't need to deny it."

"I wasn't going to." Meghan looked directly at Nina. She was a head shorter than Meghan and slightly overweight. The light-blue suit she wore was impeccable. "I think I've been in love with Thomas since I first saw him when we were in high school. Knowing that doesn't change the facts. Thomas is in love with your daughter. It doesn't matter that she died. He only needs me to give birth to her child and then my usefulness will be done."

"No disrespect to Ruth. I loved my daughter more than anything. She and Thomas were extremely happy together. But how can you accept that your usefulness will be done?"

"I don't have a choice."

"You always have a choice," she said, dismissing Meghan's comment.

Meghan moved back into the hall between the two bedrooms. "What do you suggest I do?"

"Tell him, Meghan."

"I don't think that's a good idea," Meghan said. "We have an agreement, a prenup, a surrogacy agreement and a marriage to dissolve. There's more legal paper in front of us saying this won't work than any loving couple could surmount, let alone a couple where love is unrequited."

"Meghan—"

"You can't make it happen, Nina." Meghan went to her and hugged her. "As much as you want it, you can't manipulate someone else's feelings."

Stepping back, she looked around the apartment again. "What do you think? Could you come here on rainy Sundays and tell me how he's doing?"

Nina hugged her tightly. "I can do that."

Together they pushed apart, each woman wiping mist from her eyes. "I have an idea," Nina said. "We'll go sign the papers on this apartment and then do something happy. You can decide what."

"Christmas presents," Meghan told her. "Let's go shopping."

It was snowing when Meghan came in. The house was warm and her cheeks felt instantly hot. Snow fell off her coat. The snow wouldn't last long. Too much salt from the ocean mingled with it and it melted shortly after touching the ground.

"Where were you?" Thomas asked, coming up behind her. He helped her remove her coat and hang it up.

"Walking," she said. "The air is so crisp. I would have danced circles, if I could turn circles."

They laughed. Meghan went into the music room. She felt more like she waddled. And she thought Thomas's hands were always ready to catch her if she leaned too far one way or the other.

"This is my favorite room," she said.

"I know," Thomas told her. "Since the first day you entered the house, this is where you came. That's why I put the tree in here."

"You mean, there isn't a tree in here every year?"

He shook his head. "Usually there's only the one in the living room. But I thought you'd like one in here."

The room had a warm glow to it. The lights were on because the overcast skies outside made the room dark. The tree gave the space a cheery feel. Meghan had hung holly and pine boughs about the room and the ever-present floral arrangements created a picture-perfect holiday scene. She and Thomas had decorated the tree together and while the main room's tree had many presents under it, this was the one Meghan liked and it was the one under which she'd placed his present.

Thomas loaned her his arm to help her sit down. At this stage of her pregnancy, she was awkward and found it hard to maneuver simple furniture. He dropped into the seat next to her.

"Have you finished all your shopping?"

"Finally," she said. "I know it seemed like a lot, but our old block used to get together on Christmas Eve and give each other a small present. It wasn't required, but if people could afford it, they could do something small. Once Mrs. Owens made matching bed jackets for all the women. Some of us didn't know what they were." Meghan laughed remembering that time.

"You miss them, don't you?"

"They're like family. After my parents died, the neighborhood was all we had. They helped out, supported us, gave us Christmas presents when we had none."

"They sound like wonderful people. I envy you."

"What?" Meghan turned and stared at him. "How could you envy me? You've always had everything."

"I had all the physical things."

"You parents loved you," Meghan said.

"They did. They were the best and I'm grateful they were part of my life. Nina and Adam are the salt of the earth. But you had *family,* people who looked out for you, cared about you without the customary bloodline. You're unselfish and they are unselfish in their love for you. I envy that."

Meghan's hormones kicked in at the worst times.

Her emotions rushed to her and she felt she was about to cry, but she kept the tears from falling. "I believe that is the most honest thing anyone has ever said to me."

"Are they meeting this year?"

She nodded. "It'll be at Evelyn's. I'm having a ham delivered for the party."

"Would you like to go?"

"On Christmas Eve? What about Nina and Adam? They said you always have Christmas Eve together."

"We'll take them with us, if that's all right."

Meghan threw her arms around Thomas. "I love you," she said. Thomas's hands wrapped around her large body. They stopped at her declaration. Meghan realized what she'd said. "I mean you're so good to me."

Thomas's arms went the rest of the way around her. She felt his face in her hair. He'd held her at night in bed for over a month. At times he rubbed her stomach when the baby was especially active. But he hadn't held her sexually. And Meghan craved that touch. She didn't want a doctor's hands. She wanted those of the man. She wanted the caresses and kisses. She wanted to feel the rush of anticipation and the heat of passion.

She sought his mouth as his hands skimmed over her extended belly. Pregnancy, Meghan discovered, did not dampen the flame.

It took Thomas an hour and a half to drive the distance into Baltimore every day. He'd taken the apartment in the city to avoid the drive, but he loved it now. It gave him time to get his body back in check after sleeping with Meghan in his arms and to think about her.

He filled his mind with the things she talked about. And now with the way she'd turned to him two nights ago and kissed him.

He didn't hesitate for a moment. He wanted her in his arms and his bed. He wanted her to think of him and only him. He pulled her across his lap and kissed her until he thought his body would shatter. He knew they could have sex as long as it didn't hurt her, but with a Herculean effort, he'd held back.

In bed, she'd turned into his arms when she used to lay stiff and afraid. Some nights Thomas would wake and watch her. He'd smooth her hair back and stare at her clean face. She made him feel secure, protective, loved.

Thomas hit the brake. Horns blared behind him. He looked around and continued to drive.

Loved, he thought. She made him feel loved.

He remembered the look on her face when he asked if she wanted to go back to her old neighborhood for Christmas Eve. She could have been a child seeing presents for the first time. He liked doing that for her, making her small wishes come true. He'd discovered it was the simple things that scored points with her, taking her to Christmas Eve with her friends was preferable to a diamond bracelet.

She didn't know it, but she was a diamond. And he was in love with her.

It was with this thought that Thomas entered the parking garage and rode the elevator up to his office. He felt as if he'd turned over and found a new life this morning. Meghan was part of it. Meghan was all of it.

It was Christmas Eve. She was coming in this afternoon with Nina and Adam so they could all go to the Christmas Eve party. Evelyn had been excited that she was coming and planned to keep her presence a secret from the other guests. They would all be overwhelmed to see her.

"You're going to be late for your meeting, Thomas." His secretary stood in his doorway, and he was still holding his overcoat.

"Who calls a meeting on Christmas Eve?"

"There are some people who don't know it's Christmas," she replied. "Like the ones on the conference call from Japan."

"I'll be right there." He checked his watch. He had a couple of minutes. Rhonda turned to leave. He stopped her. "As soon as the meeting is over, send everyone home. It's Christmas Eve."

Only a skeleton crew was in anyway, but Thomas knew they had families and loved ones to get to or an hour or so of last-minute shopping.

"Thanks."

He grabbed the folder that he'd studied at home and headed for the conference room. Thomas had been on teleconference for twenty minutes when Rhonda came in and handed him a paper with a single word on it.

"Emergency?" Thomas whispered, frowning at the paper. He knew she would only interrupt the meeting if it was absolutely necessary.

He looked up at her. She nodded and whispered, "Mrs. Russell is on the phone."

"Excuse me," Thomas addressed the assembly of investment professionals both in the room and a world away. "We'll have to reschedule this."

Leaving the room, forcing himself not to sprint to his office, his only thought of Meghan. What was the emergency? Was she all right? Was the baby coming early? His heart was in his throat by the time he reached his office. The room seemed to grow as he strode across the carpeted floor.

"Nina?" He spoke without a greeting. "What's wrong?"

"Meghan's gone into labor. We're at the hospital."

"It's too early."

"I know, but she was cramping when we got there and we called an ambulance," Nina said.

Thomas could hear the stress in her voice. "Is everything all right?"

"I don't know. The doctors are still examining her, but I think something is wrong, Thomas."

"I'll be right there."

Thomas shaved half an hour off the time it usually took to get to the ocean, rushing into the hospital's emergency room in a controlled, but frantic state.

"Meghan Worthington-Yates," he said to the nurse at the station. "I'm her husband."

"Thomas?" Nina and Adam came down the hall before the nurse could answer. Mrs. Barrie followed them.

"How is she?" he asked.

"We don't know." She took a moment to glance at her husband. Her face was taut and serious. "They have told us nothing. She's still in with the doctors."

"It's all right," Thomas assured them. He was

unsure himself, but he wanted to make sure his in-laws were calm.

"Is her doctor here?"

Adam nodded. "He got here just after we talked to you. He went into her room and hasn't come out."

"There's been a steady flow of people and equipment going in there." Nina's voice wavered. "Thomas, I'm scared."

"Let me find out what I can," he told them, kissing Nina on the cheek and giving Adam an assuring glance.

Leaving them, he went to the nurses' station. The woman he'd spoken to on entering looked up at him.

"Is there anything you can tell me about my wife, Mrs. Worthington-Yates?"

She punched keys on her keyboard and read a moment before looking up at him. "The doctor is still with her, but she hasn't entered her diagnosis yet."

"We're going crazy here," he said, controlling anger that was growing inside him. "I need to know something."

"Mr. Worthington-Yates?"

Thomas looked up at the sound of his name. He recognized Dr. Petry.

"Come with me," she said.

Thomas followed her down the hospital corridor. It was a place he was familiar with, having walked these halls several times with Ruth.

"Is she all right, Dr. Petry?"

"We can talk in my office," she said. "But to put your mind at ease, yes, she'll be all right. And the baby is all right, too."

Thomas thought his heart would stop. The relief was

almost physical. Thomas was grateful the doctor gestured to the chair and he dropped into it before Dr. Petry had rounded her desk and taken her seat.

"She had an episode."

"What does that mean?"

"It means premature labor. She had all the symptoms of labor, but her water has not broken. We stopped her labor."

Thomas took a long breath. He didn't know they could do that.

"We could have delivered today, but it's safer for the baby if she goes full term. At this point, her pregnancy is considered high-risk."

He was about to ask what that was when the doctor continued.

"It means she is to stay off her feet. She can go to the bathroom. She can shower sitting on a handicap chair. I don't want her going anywhere. If there are stairs, you can carry her up and down, but I suggest you make accommodations for her on the ground level."

Thomas nodded. "I'll arrange it. Is there anything else?"

"Just make sure she doesn't do anything stressful. I'm sending her home with a monitor. She's to wear it at all times. The nurse will show you how to read it and what to look for. If there is any change, even a small one, I want to know immediately."

"You can count on it," Thomas said nodding. "Can I see her?"

Dr. Petry smiled.

"One at a time." The warning note in her voice told

him she meant his in-laws and Mrs. Barrie, who'd looked just as concerned as Adam and Nina.

"Will she be able to go home today?"

"She's a strong woman, Mr. Worthington-Yates. I have every confidence she and the baby will both come through this with flying colors. I'm doing the paperwork to have her released."

"Thank you, Doctor," Thomas said, more relieved than he could ever remember being.

A nurse appeared in the door. Thomas looked up at her as Dr. Petry gave her instructions about the monitor and to take Thomas to see Meghan.

Thanking Dr. Petry again, Thomas left the room. Nina, Adam and Mrs. Barrie were a small congregation waiting for word. Briefly he stopped and reported what the doctor had said.

"Thank God," Nina said, dropping down on a bench in the hall. "Thank God, thank God, thank God," she repeated.

"I'm going to see her now. You can go in when I come out."

Adam nodded, waving him away. Thomas continued, following the nurse to emergency-room unit three.

The rush of emotion that slammed into him when he saw her would not be denied. Like a true husband, he rushed to her bed, taking her into his arms and hugging her close. He felt her warmth and heard the soft tears as she cried.

"They say the baby is all right," she told him.

"So are you," he confirmed. "You can go home as soon as they finish the paperwork, but you can't do anything."

"I know." She spoke into his shoulder. "I'm high-risk," she said. "The doctor is putting a monitor on me." She went on to tell him exactly what the doctor had already explained. Thomas let her, comforted by the soft sound of her voice, the feel of her extended belly against his side, the sureness of her presence and the knowledge that she was safe and healthy.

"Nina and Adam are in the hall. They want to see you along with Mrs. Barrie."

"I scared Mrs. Barrie. She screamed when she found me on the floor at the top of the stairs. Please tell her everything is going to be all right."

"She knows. I told them before coming in."

Pushing her back, he looked into her eyes. Her mouth quivered and he wanted to stop it with his own, but he only looked at her. Her face was pale, her eyes wide and large.

"I was so scared," she said. "What if I lost it?"

"Shh," he told her. "You didn't. There's no need to think anything like that. You're fine, the baby's fine. That's all that matters."

It took a moment, but she nodded.

"Ready for Nina to come in?"

Wiping the tears from her eyes, she nodded.

Thomas leaned forward and kissed her mouth. He couldn't stop himself. He didn't want to stop himself. He'd lain next to her night after night, wanting her, wanting her to turn to him, wrap her arms around his neck and settle into him, but she wouldn't move farther than was comfortable. Their agreement separated them. It seemed so long ago that they'd made it. However,

Meghan was a woman of integrity, and she would follow through on the terms set forth.

But he was ready to renegotiate, even if it wasn't part of her usual method of operation. Things had changed. He'd changed. She'd changed, too. And what he felt with her in his arms had to mean something. He was a good judge of character. And he knew when a woman was attracted to him.

But was it enough? Would she want to stay with him, change her plans for him? He had to find out. And he had to do it soon.

It was the worst of times. Meghan couldn't cough or sneeze or moan without someone jumping to see if she was all right. Nina brought her magazines that her constant conversation afforded Meghan no time to read. Thomas had not returned to work and when he wasn't driving her crazy he was distracting her.

He came into the music room, the place where Meghan told him she would most like to spend the day. At night Thomas carried her up to bed and brought her down in the morning.

Virtually overnight the place had been transformed. He and Mrs. Barrie had brought in everything she might need to remain comfortable and immobile.

"Mrs. Barrie sent you some tea," Thomas said. "Would you like me to pour it?"

He was dressed causally in a khaki slacks and an open-neck shirt.

"Thomas, you have got to go."

He stared at her. "Go where?"

"Back to work, anywhere. All of you need to return to whatever your routine is or was. I am not an invalid."

"You need someone with you."

"Not at all times. I am capable of being left alone. Mrs. Barrie is in the house. Nina and Adam do not need to come by every day to make sure I'm all right."

"I suppose we have been a little cloying."

"Suffocatingly close. I know you all mean well." She took the tea from him. "I promise to do what the doctor said. I will only get up when absolutely necessary and I'll have Mrs. Barrie assist me when I do."

There was a wheelchair within arm's reach. Mrs. Barrie could help her into it and roll her to the bathroom when necessary.

"If you all keep hovering, it'll be even more stressful. And you have a business to run."

"Are you sure?"

"Absolutely," she said, confidently.

"All right. I'll return in the morning, but I'm coming home every night."

Meghan nodded, smiling. She did want to see him every day. Suzanne had been right. Living with a man was vastly different from living with your sister. She loved her sister, but she was in love with her husband.

Chapter 14

For a week Thomas was constantly underfoot. Meghan could do nothing without him helping or getting it for her. It was driving her batty. No amount of pleading would sway Thomas from his role as her self-appointed guardian. He'd told Dr. Petry that he'd see that her wishes were carried out and it was like a contract written in stone. He hovered over her, carrying her down the stairs in the morning and letting her spend the day in the music room. At night he'd reverse the action and carry her to bed.

"Thomas, I understand that you're concerned about the baby," Meghan told him several days after he'd assumed the position of her nursemaid. She sat on the sofa, a wall of pillows propping her up. "But you need to go back to work."

"Suppose something happens?"

"Nothing's going to happen."

"The doctor said you're high-risk. That means something could happen."

"It won't," she said, positively. "And even if it does, you're a young man. If anything goes wrong, and I'm sure it won't, you can marry and have other children."

"I can't," he said.

"I know it won't be Ruth's child, but it'll be yours. You'll love it the same, wouldn't you?"

"Of course I would. But that's not it."

"That's not it," she repeated. Meghan stared at him. They'd been playing cards. He'd been keeping her busy, doing things she liked to do. He got up and walked away. Meghan waited for an explanation, but she didn't think one would come. Thomas looked off into space. Meghan wondered what he was thinking.

Was he still so in love with Ruth that the thought of marrying and having another child was distasteful?

Her heart hurt. She wanted to love him, wanted him to love her, but she knew Ruth was someone she could not compete with.

Then he spoke. "This is my last chance, Meghan."

His voice was so soft, she had to strain to hear him.

"Last chance for what?"

"Fatherhood. If this baby dies, I can't have any more."

"I don't understand."

He came back to the sofa and sat down. She moved her legs to accommodate him. For the first time, he didn't move to give her the benefit of comfort.

Folding his hands between his legs, he looked down for a long time. Meghan knew whatever it was, it was difficult for him to talk about. She waited, allowing him all the time he needed.

"I was driving."

She said nothing.

"Ruth died in a car accident. I was driving."

Meghan forced herself to remain still. This must have been eating at him since the accident.

"It had rained for several days. The weather had turned cold, cold and wet. Cold enough for black ice to form on the pavement. We were on our way home from a day of shopping for the nursery." He laughed, but cut it short. "I think Ruth bought out the store."

Meghan reached for his hand. He let her take it. She placed it on her stomach, even though the baby was surprisingly quiet. For a while the only sound in the room was the fetal monitor she wore.

"I lost control of the car. It spun around several times before hitting solid ground, but it was still moving forward. Ahead of us was a streetlight. I tried to swerve, but then we hit more ice and skidded. The car hit the pole and wrapped around it. Both airbags deployed. Ruth's pushed her head back. A street light fell from the pole, hitting the car and caving in the roof. It hit Ruth and broke her neck."

Meghan's hands went to her throat and she gasped.

"I was wedged behind the steering wheel unconscious and bleeding. They tell me the surgery lasted for five hours. I don't remember it. I woke up in the hospital with a neck brace on and unable to father any more children."

Meghan moved, taking his arms and pulling them around her neck.

"So you understand, this baby is my last hope."

"Thank you, Thomas," she said.

"What are you thanking me for?"

"For trusting me with this. I know it was hard for you to tell me. In all these months you've never mentioned it. Now I understand why you're so protective of me. But I promise, I'll do nothing to endanger this baby. She's a miracle child. And you deserve a miracle."

He kissed her cheek and sat back. "I'm going to get it. I'm planning on being your shadow."

"Thomas, you can't stay here for six more weeks."

"I have everything I need here."

She stared at him. He was smiling. "Who'll carry you up and down the stairs?"

"I won't need to go. I can stay here all day. Mrs. Barrie is here and if you have to work late, I can sleep here. Adam and Nina are only a short drive away. And since I missed Christmas Eve, some of my friends want to come out and visit."

"One or two at a time," he said.

"Most of them work, so they can't come until the weekend anyway."

"And I'll be here."

"You know I've never seen this military side of you."

His eyes bore directly into hers. "I'm a tyrant when it comes to protecting those I love."

The New Year dawned without incident. Meghan settled into another routine. After the steady stream of visitors died down, Thomas put a laptop computer near her so she could spend some time on the Internet. She read up on investments, trying to understand what he did.

January blended into February and the promise of spring was in the air. One more month, Meghan thought one morning as she waited for Thomas to awaken. Her body had grown to whale status. She passed rhino a couple of months back. She lay in bed with his comforting hand on her hip. He liked touching her.

Even though her ability to sleep had decreased in the last few weeks, she didn't leave the bed until he was awake to help her.

Suddenly she jerked. The baby kicked. This one was harder than any of the previous ones. Only another month, she told it silently. You can join the world soon. Another one came, this time accompanied by a hard pain in her abdomen. She grunted hard.

Thomas opened his eyes and sat up. "What is it?"

"I don't know. I thought it was just... Owww!" she screamed.

They had both attended child birth classes and this was nothing like what Meghan had been led to expect.

"Meghan, talk to me," he ordered. She felt he was damping down his concern.

She took several deep breaths. "I think this is a labor pain."

"It's too early. You have another month."

"I knooooow," she said, blending the word into the pain that caught her.

"They're coming too fast," Thomas said.

He jumped out of bed and grabbed his pants as he ran into the hall. "Mrs. Barrie," was all Meghan heard him shout before she was gripped with another pain. She felt like Thomas had been gone hours when he came back. Meghan could only moan in pain.

"This isn't how it's supposed to be."

"We're going to the hospital."

Meghan bit her lip trying not to cry out in pain. She could see the hurt on Thomas's face each time she hurt. Again the pain gripped her. Thomas lifted her, still dressed in her bedclothes, and carried her from the room.

Mrs. Barrie was in the garage when they got there. He put Meghan in the backseat and stood up.

"Get in with her," Mrs. Barrie said. "I'm driving."

Thomas didn't argue with the housekeeper. He got in and she backed out of the garage.

Meghan clutched her stomach and Thomas during the eternity it took to get to the hospital. He kept talking to her, whispering quietly in her ear. She was in too much pain to understand his words, but she knew they were comforting.

Finally, the pain began to subside. She was hot, sweaty, suddenly cold. She slumped against Thomas. Mrs. Barrie jumped out of the car in the emergency lane.

"I don't feel good," she told Thomas.

"Just hang on, honey. Help is here." His arms tightened around her and he kissed her damp forehead.

"I think…I think the pain. It's receding." Meghan could hardly hear her own voice. Her head felt funny. Dizzy. "Thomas…wrong." She couldn't get her words out.

The door was yanked open. Meghan squinted at the sun's glare. Her arms were suddenly heavy.

"Turn this way, Mrs. Worthington." Someone spoke from behind her. Meghan wanted to tell her that wasn't her name. She couldn't move. She was too tired. Her lids closed.

"Meghan," Thomas called her name.

She made a noise and raised her hand, but it fell back.

"Meghan!"

She felt Thomas was shouting at her, but the blackness that closed around her dragged her down with it. His voice got softer and softer.

And then it was gone.

If he'd had the presence of mind to think about what was happening, he'd commend the hospital staff for the way they flew into action, but he was too busy shouting, "What's wrong with her?"

They didn't know and Thomas refused to leave Meghan's side. Finally, a huge orderly came in and threatened to carry him away if he didn't leave.

He went to back to the waiting area. Mrs. Barrie stood up the moment she saw him.

"How is she?"

He took her hands. They were cold. Thomas realized Mrs. Barrie was truly concerned about Meghan.

"They're still trying to figure out what's wrong."

"I saw Dr. Petry come in," Mrs. Barrie said. "She hurried through that door."

Thomas followed the line of her finger. The door led to the area where Meghan had been wheeled.

"Can I get you something? You haven't had anything to eat since last night."

"Thank you, no." Thomas walked to the end of the small room. The furniture was slightly upgraded from most hospitals. The magazines in the waiting room were less than a year old. Thomas looked at none of them. He paced back and forth, continually looking for Dr. Petry to appear and tell him Meghan was going to be all right.

Fifteen minutes went by. Mrs. Barrie came back carrying a cup of coffee and two slices of buttered toast. She insisted Thomas eat them. He had no memory of tasting them, but they were gone half an hour later.

"What is taking so long?" he asked, speaking more to himself that asking a question.

"I'm sure she'll be all right," she reassured him.

Thomas left the room and went to the nurses' station.

"Could you check on my wife, please?" The woman sitting at the desk wore a pink and white cotton tunic.

"What is her name?"

Thomas answered her questions and she typed the information into the computer. "There's no report yet," she said, standing up. "Let me check and see what I can find out."

He drummed his fingers on the counter while he waited for her to return. When she did, Dr. Petry was with her. The nurse pointed to Thomas and Dr. Petry came toward him. There was no smile on her face. Thomas knew something had gone wrong.

"I want to see her," he said as soon as the doctor was within earshot.

Dr. Petry was dwarfed by Thomas's tall, imposing stature, yet she took his arm and propelled him into a staff office.

"I want to know what's going on," he said.

"The truth is we don't know what's going on.

Meghan's blood pressure dropped suddenly. That's why she passed out. We're doing everything we can right now."

"What about the baby?"

"She's in distress. The baby is in distress."

Dr. Petry was not one to mince words. Thomas had always liked that about her. But right now he wasn't sure what he wanted to know. Fear gripped him. He had the awful feeling that something was seriously wrong.

"I want to see her."

"She's not awake."

"What?"

Dr. Petry took a deep breath. "She's in a coma."

Thomas thought his legs would give out. Mrs. Barrie's breath caught in her throat.

"Coma? What could cause her to be in a coma?"

"Thomas, we don't know," Dr. Petry said. "We're doing everything we can."

"Can't you bring her out of it?"

"We're not sure that's the right course of action yet."

Thomas clinched his teeth and tried to calm himself. "What is the course of action?"

She took his arm then. "Call Meghan's sister and tell her to get on the first plane."

Thomas fell into a chair. "She's not going to die," he said. "She's not going to die." This time his voice was stronger. He was shouting at Dr. Petry. She didn't move or try to stop him.

This was not real. Thomas stared at Dr. Petry as she'd just given his latest prognosis. Stunned, he could hardly move. He'd been in the hospital two days, rarely leaving Meghan's side. She lay silently in a hospital bed, her face pale against the stark whiteness of the sheets. Nina and Adam tried to get him to leave, but he stayed, only taking short forays home to shower and shave. Mrs. Barrie brought him food, which he either didn't eat or didn't remember eating.

Meghan's condition hadn't changed. Dr. Petry had given him regular updates until this morning when she'd given him more bad news.

Meghan lay sleeping. It wasn't a normal sleep and it scared Thomas. He'd never been so scared in his life. Nothing else mattered except her. He loved her. He needed her, needed her goodness, her kind and unselfish heart. He needed her understanding and her gentle touch.

He stood up. Nina and Adam were outside and he needed to speak to them.

They stood the moment he came to the waiting room. Nina didn't look as sharply pressed as she usually did, but then again none of them looked as put together as they usually did. They had all been here before. When Ruth died, he imagined they'd had the same haggard expressions.

"Is there any change?" Nina asked.

"Dr. Petry left a few minutes ago. There isn't much time."

"No," Nina cried. She clutched her heart. Tears sprang to her eyes and ran down her cheeks. Adam turned her into his shoulder.

"They are going to have to take the baby."

"Will she be all right?"

"We don't know." Thomas hesitated. He was working hard to keep his emotions in check. He didn't know how long he could keep it up. He was about to lose another wife. "They don't know if either of them will survive."

"No!" The voice came from the doorway. All eyes turned to see Suzanne standing there with Mrs. Barrie. "What do you mean?"

Thomas went to his sister-in-law and hugged her. She pushed out of his arms. "Explain what you meant."

He briefly went through Meghan's condition as it stood now.

"She can't die." Her eyes darted to the people around the room. They all stood as still as statues. "She never wanted to have children. You've got to tell them to save her." Her hands grabbed his arms.

Thomas pulled her into his arms. "I love her. She's my first priority. If there is a choice, it's Meghan."

He stared at his in-laws over Suzanne's head. Their faces looked stunned, but both of them nodded.

"Where is she?"

"Mrs. Barrie?" Without him voicing the request, Mrs. Barrie understood and took Suzanne down the hall to the room where her sister slept.

When the door closed, he turned back to his in-laws. "Meghan never wanted to have children," he said. "She told me. Now she's in danger of losing her life because she's having my child. I can't let her die. It would be like dying myself."

"Of course you can't," Adam said.

Nina came to him. "We understand. We love her, too."

"It's not that I don't love Ruth," he said.

Nina put her hand to his mouth to stop him. "You don't have to say it. We know. Ruth was lucky to have you. You made her happy. If her life was cut short, we're glad she knew happiness before she died."

"But Ruth's gone now," Adam took up the conversation as if he and Nina were of the same mind. "You're alive. Meghan is alive. And you love each other. That's all that counts."

"Meghan doesn't love me," he contradicted.

"I think you're wrong there," Adam said. Nina only smiled, even through the tears in her eyes. "Take my word for it, Thomas. No woman could look at you the way she does and not be in love."

Thomas looked from one to the other. "I didn't know." And now he wondered if he'd get the chance to tell her.

They were wheeling Meghan out when Thomas got to her room. Suzanne and Mrs. Barrie supported each other near the door. He caught up with the bed and took her hand. He wasn't leaving her. He was going to be there until all was done.

"Thomas…" Her voice had the impact of dropping a nuclear bomb.

"Stop!" he commanded the orderly. The wheels came to a halt silent on the rubber floor.

"Where are we going? I'm thirsty."

Thomas hadn't cried since he was seven years old, but tears rushed into his eyes and fell unchecked down his face. She reached up and touched them.

"You're crying," she said incredulously. "Are you all right?"

He laughed through the tears.

"We have to go," the orderly said.

Thomas nodded. He kept hold of Meghan's hand and smiled at her as they went into the operating room. Thomas was dressed in a blue-green smock before he went into the theater.

Dr. Petry was talking to Meghan when Thomas was considered clean enough to enter the theater.

"She's awake for now. The numbness and anesthesia should kick in soon." Dr. Petry smiled at Thomas.

He went to his place near Meghan's head. "How is she?"

"I don't know. We'll have to check her vitals and the baby's, make sure everything is all right before we can proceed." She looked at Meghan. "It appears this little kid is defying all odds."

"She's a miracle baby," Meghan said.

Chapter 15

"It's a boy." Thomas burst into the waiting room with the news. "Eight pounds, five ounces, twenty-three inches long, a full head of black hair."

A sigh of relief went through the family, then happiness brought smiles to their faces.

"Meghan?" Suzanne asked, her chin trembling.

"She's fine," Thomas said, going to her. "Mother and child are doing well." Suzanne looked pale, stunned, frozen. She fell into the chair and wept. "Don't cry, Suzanne. It's a joyous day."

Suzanne tried to smile. "I was so scared."

"I understand," Thomas told her. "I've never been so scared in my life."

"But it all worked out," Nina said. "She's going to be fine."

"Can I see her?"

"As soon as she gets to her room, which won't be long. She's very tired, but she's going to be fine."

"I can't stop crying," Suzanne said.

"Go ahead. You've earned the right."

Instead of crying, Suzanne laughed.

Thomas laughed, too. "The baby is in the nursery. Why don't you all go see the newest member of the family? He'll be easy to find. He's the best looking child there."

Meghan felt as if she'd spent a lifetime away from this house. Funny, she thought, looking around the bedroom she'd shared with Thomas, she'd only lived here for nine months, yet she thought of this place as home. It wasn't. As of today, she no longer lived here.

The separation was already happening. In the hospital, Meghan had had the child to herself. Thomas held him during his visits, but hospital policy only allowed for the parents to lift and hold the child. She was back now and she could barely hold him. Nina and Adam were so thrilled with their grandchild that they never let her do anything. Suzanne delighted in being an aunt. Meghan didn't think her sister remembered that she and the child shared no bloodline.

Meghan felt an allegiance to the baby. She'd carried him for nine months, felt him growing inside her. It was hard to think of him as someone else's baby. Yet he wasn't hers.

Meghan opened the suitcase from the hospital. Her nightgown, slippers, toothbrush stared at her. Each item told her that her duties here were done. It was time to fulfill the agreement and move into her apartment. It was ready. She'd had her things moved from storage. She could go there tonight. Of course, she'd have to pick up some food, but that would be a minor glitch in the scheme of things. And right now she wasn't hungry. Maybe she wouldn't be tonight, either.

Going to the dresser, she removed her clothes and put them in the suitcase. She continued, moving back and forth until the bag was packed.

Her second suitcase was in the other room, the room she used to sleep in before Thomas carried her to his bed and kept her there. She turned to go and get it. And jumped.

"How long have you been standing there?" Meghan asked Thomas. He leaned against the doorjamb, watching her. A smile curved his lips.

"Not long. What are you doing?"

"Packing."

"Why?"

"You know why."

"No, I don't."

"Contract terms, Thomas. Remember them. I have a baby, then I get an apartment and I go to school."

"Just like that?"

"What does that mean?"

"How can you walk away from your son without a backward glance? What kind of mother are you?"

Meghan burst into tears. She turned away from him, but he was instantly at her side. He took her shoulders and turned her into his arms.

"Meghan, I was kidding. I didn't mean to make you cry."

"Its hormones," she lied. She loved that baby. And she loved his father. And walking out the door was going to be the hardest thing she'd ever done.

"You can't go," he said.

"What?" She leaned back, hope trying to get a foothold in her heart. She forced it back in place.

"I love you. I've been telling you for days, but you couldn't hear me. I'm not letting you go."

"What about our deal?"

"Be damned with it. When I thought I might lose you, I didn't know how I would go on living. I wanted you more than anything in the world. And I'm not losing you over some agreement."

"You're playing with my head." Meghan stared at him. Waiting. This had to be a joke. He had to be kidding. His face didn't move. She kept staring at him, wondering when the edges of his mouth would turn up and he'd laugh at her discomfort. It was a game of chicken.

Meghan smiled, then laughed. Thomas's expression remained unchanged.

"You're not kidding," she stated.

"Do you love me?"

Meghan didn't know what to say. She decided on the truth. "More than anything."

"I love you, too."

"And when two people love each other, they become a family. I want you in my life. I want you in my family."

"What about your son?"

"He's not my son. He's *our* son."

Meghan threw her arms around him. "Do you mean that? I love you. And I love our son."

Thomas kissed her. Meghan kissed him back. His arms tightened around her. They remained that way for a long time.

"I think we should go downstairs and tell Nina and Adam that they have a daughter-in-law," Thomas said. "And let Suzanne know she's officially an aunt."

Meghan nodded. As they reached the door, she stopped. Thomas looked at her, a question in his dark, sexy eyes. She went to the dresser. Her wedding rings lay there. They had been removed in the hospital and Mrs. Barrie had brought them home.

Thomas picked them up. Taking her left hand, he slipped the rings in place.

"Forever and a day," he said, then sealed the promise with a kiss.

A love that's out of this world…

Cosmic Rendezvous

Favorite author

Robyn Amos

For aerospace engineer Shelly London, a top-secret
space project could be her big break—until she butts
heads with sexy hotshot astronaut Lincoln Ripley, who
launches her hormones right into orbit. Lincoln's got
a double mission: catch a saboteur…then take off with
Shelly for a rendezvous with love.

"Lilah's List is…a fun story that
holds one's interest from page one."
—*Romantic Times BOOKreviews*

*Coming the first week of April 2009
wherever books are sold.*

KIMANI™
ROMANCE

The "Triple Threat" Donovan brothers are back…
and last-man-standing Trent is about to roll the
dice on falling in love.

Defying DESIRE

Book #3 in *The Donovan Brothers*

A.C. Arthur

When it comes to men, model Tia St. Claire wants no
strings, just flings. But navy SEAL Trent Donovan stirs
defiant longings she can't deny. Happily unattached,
Trent has dedicated his career to duty and danger, until
desire—and Tia—changes everything.

"If hero Adam Donovan was for sale, every woman in
the world would be lined up to buy him!"
—*Romantic Times BOOKreviews* on
A CINDERELLA AFFAIR

*Coming the first week of April 2009
wherever books are sold.*

KIMANI™
ROMANCE

He's an irresistible recipe—for trouble!

Sugar RUSH

elaine overton

Life is sweet for bakery owner Sophie Mayfield.
She's saved her family business from a takeover, and
hired talented baker Eliot Wright to help sales. Eliot
is as appealing—and oh-so-chocolate-fine—as he is
hardworking. But when Sophie discovers Eliot is not
what he seems, Eliot must regain Sophie's trust—and
prove he's her permanent sweet spot.

*Coming the first week of April 2009
wherever books are sold.*

KIMANI™
ROMANCE

KPEO110409

REQUEST YOUR FREE BOOKS!

2 FREE NOVELS
PLUS 2 FREE GIFTS!

KIMANI
ROMANCE
™

Love's ultimate destination!

A dazzling story of a woman forced to decide where her heart really lies…

AWARD-WINNING AUTHOR

ADRIANNE BYRD

Love
takes time

All her life, Alyssa Jansen has loved handsome, wealthy Quentin Dwayne Hinton—a man who barely knows she exists. Now after years away in France, Alyssa's back, and Q is seeing her in a whole new light. But so is his brother Sterling, a handsome and passionate man who is willing to give Alyssa what she wants. Suddenly Alyssa must choose between a fairy tale come true and a new, unexpected love….

Coming the first week of April 2009 wherever books are sold.

ARABESQUE®

NEW YORK TIMES BESTSELLING AUTHOR

BRENDA JACKSON

SURRENDER

A Madaris Family Novel

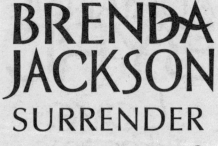

Military brat Nettie Brooms has vowed never to become involved with a military man. But Ashland Sinclair, a marine colonel, has very different ideas about the sexy restaurant owner. Now Nettie's wondering how a man she swore she would avoid could so easily test her resolve by igniting a passion she can't walk away from.

Available the first week of April 2009 wherever books are sold.

ARABESQUE®